THE GREEN YEARS

(Jute, Jam & Jiving through Dundee)

by

Sandra Savage

Copyright © Sandra Savage 2016

This book is sold subject to the condition that it shall not, by way of trade or otherwise, be lent, resold, hired out, or otherwise circulated without the publisher's prior consent in any form of binding or cover other than that in which it is published and without a similar condition including this condition being imposed on the subsequent publisher.
The moral right of Sandra Savage has been asserted.

Acknowledgements

In memory of Grace Campbell who passed away in 2015. Always remembered for her kindness and generosity.

Also by Sandra Savage

Annie Pepper

Annie Melville

Annie MacPherson

The Pepper Girls

The Dark Heart of Roger Lomax

Chapter 1

The Fintry bus squelched to a stop, splashing black water onto the shoes of Maisie Green. It was Friday and she'd just finished another week at Keiller's Factory, packing chocolates into boxes for delivery to the many Dundee sweetie shops.

She boarded the bus and gave the conductor a raised eyebrow as she indicated her shoes and stockings dotted with the muddy water.

"Should 've stood away from the kerb," he shouted after her, grinning at her annoyance, as she climbed the steep steps to the top deck where she could have a 'ciggie.' The atmosphere up top was hazy with tobacco smoke as she took her seat amongst the busload of coughing and wheezing passengers.

She lit up her Senior Service fag and inhaled deeply, but Maisie had only one thing on her mind and that was the up-coming works dance and Kenny Wilson. Kenny worked in the Sugar Boiling Room and was the best looking guy around. With his Elvis quiff and broad shoulders, he had Maisie smitten, like most of the other girls at Keiller's. At 20 years of age, Kenny was dreamily known as a 'real man'.

The bumpy journey from Reform Street to her home in Fintry flew by as she pictured herself in the arms of Kenny, cheek to cheek in a 'moondance', as all the other girls watched jealously from the balcony of Kidds Ballroom. Bliss!

The fact that Kenny Wilson had barely noticed Maisie at all didn't hinder her desire for him and, in her young mind, it was only a matter of time anyway, before he realised that she was 'the one.'

She hurried up the path and unlocked the door. "Anybody in?" she called, but there was no response. There was, however, a note on the mantelpiece from her mother.

At Bingo with Ella Henderson, it read. Wallaces Bridie in oven just heat. Leave board money in tin on shelf. Mum.

Maisie looked round her home. The Green's bland living room held a Brown Rexine settee, a couple of brown fireside chairs, a dining table and sideboard and a new television in the corner, which seemed somehow out of place amongst all the brown furniture.

It was cold too in the house and she switched on a bar of the electric fire, which sat in the now defunct coal fireplace, before heading into the kitchen and her Bridie. As soon as she'd eaten, she'd go round to Chrissie's house to discuss 'things' about the dance and Kenny Wilson.

Chrissie was Maisie's best friend. There was nothing they couldn't talk about and at 16 years of age, of course, both girls knew EVERYTHING about boys!

Chrissie Dalton was a Packer, like Maisie, and both girls had worked in Keiller's since leaving Stobswell Girls School the year before. With only basic qualifications, the other options open to them were shop work at 'Woollies' or in the jute mills.

"No contest," Chrissie had said, "and all the 'choccies' you can eat!"

It was a five minute walk to Chrissie's house in Fintry and Maisie hurried through the increasing drizzle, head down and a flimsy red chiffon scarf covering her beehive hairdo.

Should have brought an umbrella, she chided herself, but decided there was enough lacquer on her hair to keep it in place till she got to Chrissie's.

She hurried up the garden path and knocked. Almost instantly, Chrissie opened the door. "Hurry up," she whispered, "dad's watchin' fitba' on the telly and he's not in a good mood. United's not doing too great."

The two girls tiptoed past the living room door and upstairs into Chrissie's room.

"First things first," said Maisie, "I need some lacquer."

Chrissie looked at the rather lop-sided hairdo and nodded.

"Is that hair going to be alright for the dance the morn?"

Maisie grabbed the lacquer and started spraying it over her hair, pushing the beehive gently from one side in an attempt to straighten it up. "There," she said satisfied with the result, "now the next thing is a ciggie."

Chrissie obliged and the two friends lit up, blowing smoke into the air in a sophisticated manner, copying the film stars they'd seen at the pictures.

Very soon, the talk turned to Kenny Wilson and the chances of Maisie winning his heart at Keiller's dance.

"I'm more interested in Rab Skelly," said Chrissie wistfully, "he's no' as good looking as Kenny," she conceded, but he's got really bonnie eyes."

"Well," Maisie countered quickly, wishing to turn the conversation back to Kenny and herself, "you can have Rab and I'll have Kenny," she concluded. "Agreed?" Chrissie nodded vigorously.

"Now," Maisie asked, "what are you wearing?"

Chrissie frowned. "There's not much choice," she said as she rummaged through the small built-in wardrobe that held her entire range of fashion items. "There's this frock," she announced, holding up a sleeveless dress of pale green crimpolene with a hem that needed stitching and a faint underarm stain. "No, too plain," Maisie advised, subtly.

"Then, how about this," she said, producing a pink satin brocade dress she'd worn as a bridesmaid at her sister's wedding.

"Better," said Maisie, cautiously, "but it's a bit..... BIG". Chrissie eyed the bulky brocade number that almost stood up on its own and duly returned it to the wardrobe.

"Well," she decided, "it'll have to be the black pencil skirt and the flowery blouse," she bemoaned. "It's all there is left!"

Maisie nodded wisely. "Good choice," she said.

"And what about yourself," Chrissie asked, "what are you wearing?"

Maisie propped up her chin with her hands as she lay face down on Chrissie's bed. She too didn't have much choice of 'evening wear', not like the lassies from Keiller's offices, who seemed to be wearing a different outfit every time she saw them, as they sauntered through the factory on their way to and from their offices.

"Well?" Chrissie repeated.

Maisie sat up and lit another cigarette. "I've seen this brilliant frock in Paiges and it'll be just perfect." She warmed to her topic. "It's sleeveless, black with a yellow and orange flame-like pattern 'round the hem, but....."

Chrissie waited, "but I need a decent pair of black stilettos to go with it." She looked beseechingly at her friend. "You wouldn't happen to have a pair, would you?"

Chrissie pursed her lips. "You know fine, I've got a pair, you were with me when I bought them at Birrells last week."

Maisie pretended ignorance.

"Was I?"

Chrissie produced the box with the shoes, black patent leather with a bow on the front. Maisie's eyes lit up covetously, wondering what inducement she could offer in exchange for the perfect shoes.

"You could have my circular skirt for the dance if you like," Maisie said, "the one with the poppies on it."

Chrissie beamed. That would be better than the pencil skirt and the poppies would go well with the flowery blouse.

"Done," she said, packing the shoes back into their box and handing it to Maisie.

Things were looking good. "Meet me outside Paiges tomorrow at ten and I'll bring the skirt with me."

So, it was agreed, both girls happy with the swap and each already dreaming of the big night. They had a last smoke, before Maisie left for home, clutching the shoebox tightly to her and running all the way, as the drizzle worsened into a downpour.

The lights were on and the door unlocked when Maisie returned home. Her mother was watching the telly but switched it off when her daughter came into the room.

With hands on her hips and a fag on her lips, she confronted her daughter.

"Do you think we're made o' money?" she asked a puzzled Maisie.

"No?"

"Then how did you manage to leave the fire on again when you went out?"

Maisie flinched. "Forgot," she said lamely, her face flushing with guilt.

"And," her irate mother continued, shaking the empty tin in front of Maisie, "where's your board money?"

"Sorry," she said, "forgot again," as she rummaged for her purse in her handbag, extracting £2 and giving it to her mother.

Mrs Green shook her head, sending cigarette ash floating down onto the carpet below and turned back to the television, switching it on and settling down again in her chair.

Maisie slipped out of the room and upstairs to her bedroom. She knew things were hard since her dad had injured his back and had to give up work, but she soon put the thought from her head, tomorrow was her big chance with Kenny Wilson and tonight she would dream of how wonderful it was all going to be.

-----oOo-----

Chapter 2

Maisie was waiting outside Paiges Dress Shop for Chrissie to arrive. There it was, in the window, theeeee dress that would win the heart of Kenny Wilson. Maisie was lost in her reverie when Chrissie tapped her on the shoulder, excitement evident in her eyes.

"Guess who I've just seen," she giggled, "only Kenny Wilson and Rab Skelly." Chrissie went on rapidly, "they were coming out of Jacksons Tailors and they had on black drape jackets with a bit of velvet round the collar and tight, tight drainpipes." Chrissie clasped her hands and looked skywards, "and Rab had blue suede beetle-crushers on."

Maisie looked towards the Murraygate in anticipation of seeing her 'beloved' but the lads had disappeared.

"C'mon," she said, "let's buy that frock."

The shop girl was small and very neat and smiled as she removed the dress from the window and presented it to Maisie.

"It's all the rage," she said eagerly, indicating the sweetheart neckline and full skirt. "And it's the last one in the shop," she added, "you're lucky it's not been sold."

"Size 16," Maisie read, in a disappointed voice, "but I'm only a 14!"

The assistant held the dress up against Maisie, "nothing a wee bit of padding wouldn't change," she said, winking. "Everybody's doing it nowadays."

Maisie and Chrissie exchanged glances. "Really?"

The girl nodded knowingly and pointed to her own pert bosom.

"A couple of wee shoulder pads will do the trick," she advised them, "tucked into your bra."

Maisie got the picture. "I'll take it," she announced boldly. How would Kenny be able to resist her, with a bust like Diana Dors."

The girls hurried from the shop giggling at their bravado.

"Are you really going to do it Maisie?"

"You'll just have to wait and see," she replied coyly, wondering herself how she would look.

"Come round at six o'clock," Maisie said "and tonight, we'll show them office lassies from Keiller's what sex appeal is all about."

Chrissie giggled louder. "See you at six," she called, heading off to Woolworths to buy a new 'lippie', "and thanks for the skirt."

"It's only me," Maisie called as she popped her head round the living room door and held up the shop bag. Her mother turned to her daughter and tutted.

"Wasting more money," she said dismissively, turning back to the telly and the hunched back of her husband, who sat silently selecting horses to bet on, at that day's racing at Ayr.

Maisie shrugged. How could her mother possibly understand the importance of the contents of Paiges bag, she'd never been in love, except maybe with the Bingo.

She ran upstairs, unpacked her purchase and met her first problem. She had NO shoulder pads! She searched through the chest of drawers without luck then tried the wardrobe, but the only shoulder pads she could find were sewn into her only winter coat. They were a bit big and would have to be taken out from under the lining, but they'd have to do. Maisie began the unpicking. With great difficulty and a good deal of manoeuvring, Maisie finally managed to force the wide white shoulder pads out of the coat and inside her bra. The results were amazing. She stood in front of the wardrobe mirror as two round orbs appeared over the top of her bra. She had a cleavage!

Carefully, she slipped the dress over her lacquered head and allowed it to settle over her hips. It was a bit loose from the waist down, but up top....WOW! Tonight she was going to be a sensation.

By the time six o'clock came round, Maisie was ready for anything, hair perfect, makeup perfect, shoes perfect, dress nearly perfect and cleavage stunning. She couldn't wait to see Kenny Wilson's face when he saw her wonderfulness.

She wrapped her cream duster coat over the dress before answering Chrissie's knock.

"Well?" asked her friend, eagerly, "are they......?"

"You'll see," came the coy reply, "when we get to Kidds."

By the time the bus had disgorged the pair at their destination, Dundee was getting into full Saturday night swing. Teddy boys were everywhere, hanging around the street corners eyeing up the girls as they flounced past in their high heels and swirling skirts, on their way to the night's dancing at the JM Ballroom or the Palais, but for Maisie and Chrissie, there was only one place to be and that was Kidds Ballroom and Keiller's Dance.

The marble entrance was crowded with office girls in taffetta evening dresses and men in suits all heading for the cloakrooms and the bar respectively.

The girls went to check their coats into the cloakroom and it was only then that Chrissie saw the mounds of flesh that were Maisie's bosoms.

Chrissie clamped her hand over her mouth to stop her from squealing at the sight. "They're enormous," she breathed loudly, drawing attention to Maisie from the other girls in the queue, as she blushed with embarrassment.

"Over there," she instructed Chrissie in panic, before anymore eyes could turn in Maisie's direction, "upstairs to the balcony,"

By the time the girls had reached the balcony, which ran above the dance floor and held seating and the bar, Maisie had regained her composure.

She flounced into one of the chairs and Chrissie sat opposite. She couldn't take her eyes of Maisie's cleavage. "Shoulder pads," she whispered in awe, "well, who'd have thought."

"Ssssshhhh," Maisie hissed, "I don't want everybody to know."

"Sorry," Chrissie said, "it's just they're so BIG!"

From nowhere, Shug Reilly appeared at the girls table, leaning forward and gazing at Maisie's upper body. Shug worked in the Transport Department, loading boxes packed with jars of butterscotch sweeties, onto the delivery vans and carrying out all the heavy work that required 'muscle.'

"Get you lassies a drink?" he asked, his eyes never leaving Maisie's frontage. "Are you speaking to me," Maisie asked, derisively, "or just chewing a wasp?" Shug eventually met her eyes.

"No need to be like that," he said, feigning hurt at the dismissal of his offer.

"I'll have a Pink Lady," piped up Chrissie, boldly "and Maisie likes a Babycham," hoping nobody would notice they were 'underage.'

The Green Years

He turned his attention to Chrissie. "Now that's more like it," he said, "an' we'll maybe have a wee dance later," he smiled, "that's if your pal doesn't mind."

Maisie shrugged, "no skin off my nose," she countered, "and the next time you speak to me, speak to my face and not my chest."

"Don't flatter yourself Maisie Green," he tossed back, "plenty more where you've come from. Wintry Fintry isn't it?" he added, grinning, "a bit like yourself."

Shug returned to the bar and the nudges of half a dozen of his mates, but the drinks duly arrived.

Maisie looked round the balcony. Where was Kenny, she fretted, taking in the flat wooden boards packed with Keiller's pies ready for heating for the buffet later and leaned over the rail as the Johnny Hart Combo started their set.

"C'mon," she said, "we'll not get any dances sitting up here and it doesn't look like Shug's going to send over any more drinks."

Downstairs in the main ballroom the atmosphere was electric.

Dancers were pairing up and men's jackets and ties were being shrugged off as the atmosphere heated up. Johnny Hart knew his stuff and pretty soon, everyone was on the dance floor with Maisie and Chrissie jiving with the best of them. But there was still no sign of Kenny, or for that matter, Rab Skelly.

Disappointment was beginning to settle onto the shoulders of the girls when Johnny Hart grabbed the microphone and with a roll of the drums, announced that the next dance would be a 'ladies selection dance.' The girls looked bemused.

Johnny Hart continued. "During this next dance, the Departmental Managers will be choosing their best looking girls to go forward to be Miss Keiller's 1962." Everyone cheered.

"And," he finished with a bow, "as we couldn't get Tommy Steele, I will be your judge." With that the music struck up and all the girls rushed onto the floor to jive to 'Rock Around the Clock.'

Maisie feigned disinterest as the office secretaries and typists were tapped on the shoulders by their bosses, till suddenly, the Packing Department Manager, Willie Pratt, tapped her shoulder. "You're lookin' lovely as usual," he leered, his eyes never leaving Maisie's bustline, "time to show these fancy bints from the offices a thing or two," and with a knowing wink, he strolled back to the side of the dance floor.

Chrissie tried to hide her disappointment at not being 'selected' but soon brightened up when she spotted Kenny and Rab watching the 'action' from the sidelines, each with a pint of beer in their hands.

"They're here," she shouted to Maisie above the racket of the Combo's drummer, subtly indicating with a tilt of her head the spot by the entrance where the lads stood.

The music stopped with a clash of symbols and everyone cheered as the unlucky girls left the floor and the 'chosen ones' lined up in front of the stage.

Maisie felt uncomfortably conspicuous as the eyes of Johnny Hart roamed over her and the other girls, occasionally involving the audience with a wide grin and a 'thumbs up' till all the contestants had been given the once over.

The girls were whittled down to the last ten and with a further roll of the drums Johnny made his announcement.

"In third place," he drawled, "we have the Clerkess from the Wages Department, Miss Lillian Beatty." There was a polite ripple of applause as the crowd waited for the winner to be announced. "In second place," he continued, building the suspense, "we have the voluptuous Chocolate Packer, Miss Maisie Green." There was suddenly a tremendous roar and whistles from the watching lads, including Kenny Wilson, who couldn't believe he hadn't noticed Maisie Green before. He'd have to correct that, and soon.

Maisie couldn't believe it. She was runner up to Miss Keiller and smiled shyly as she was presented with a small bouquet of flowers and a box of Keiller's Continental Chocolates.

"And the winner of Miss Keiller 1962, the Secretary to Mr Keiller himself................" another roll of drums, "is Miss Catriona McPhee."

Catriona donned her sash and crown and was immediately whisked away to be photographed for the Works Magazine, while Maisie and Lillian Beatty faded into the background.

Chrissie rushed over to her. "You should've won," she said stoutly, "you're far better looking than Catriona McPhee."

But Maisie was quite happy with her second place. Kenny Wilson had been there to see her in all her glory. Surely now, he'd notice her.

-----oOo-----

Chapter 3

The excitement of the Miss Keiller Beauty Competition calmed down as the dancers were treated to a few 'slow numbers' courtesy of Johnny Hart and his boys. The ballroom lights were dimmed and a blue spotlight flickered over the dancers, as the band struck up the soulful strains of 'Blue Moon.'

Kenny and Rab didn't waste any more time as they moved, as one, through the crowd, Rab taking the arm of Chrissie and Kenny circling Maisie's shoulder with his left arm as he removed the chocolates and flowers and placed them on a nearby table with his right. "I believe this is my dance," he told Maisie rather than asked her.

Maisie turned to find Chrissie, but she'd already gone onto the dance floor with Rab. "I believe it is," said Maisie with a nod, allowing her escort to guide her onto the floor, then, without a word, he pulled her in close to him and, just like in her dreams, they began to dance, cheek to cheek. Maisie was in heaven.

As the music faded and Maisie made to leave the floor, a smug Shug Riley tapped her on the shoulder. "I believe this is yours?" he said, holding up a large white shoulder pad, "it fell from underneath your frock a minute ago." Maisie froze, at the sight of her 'falsie' in Shug's hand. All eyes, including Kenny's were suddenly fixed on the front of Maisie's frock and her lop-sided bustline.

The Green Years

Chrissie, who was watching the scene unfold from the side of the dance floor, came to the rescue. Snatching the shoulder pad from Shug's hand, she guided Maisie away from the two men who were now sniggering and pointing at her distress.

"C'mon," she said, "let's get you to the Ladies."

Through a shimmer of tears, Maisie removed the remaining padding and watched as the front of her frock collapsed back to flat.

There were nudges and winks from the other girls as they whispered that Maisie shouldn't have come second in the Miss Keiller's competition, the wee cheat.

"Let's go home," Maisie said in a shaky voice. "My life's over," she added dramatically, knowing that she could never face Kenny Wilson again.

The cold air helped to blow away the burning in Maisie's cheeks, as the two girls walked to the bus stop, Chrissie's arm linked into her friend's in a show of support.

"He's no' worth the bother," she said, stoutly, "if he'd been a real man, he would've belted Shug Reilly for embarrassing you like that."

Maisie nodded tight lipped, wishing she'd never tried to be anything other than herself. "It wasn't Shug's fault," she said, "it was my own daft fault for thinking that I could get away with fooling Kenny Wilson into thinking I was Diana Dors."

The tempting smell of chips cooking wafted into the nostrils of Maisie and Chrissie, as they neared the mobile Chip Shop at the corner of the Overgate. It was doing a roaring trade as hunger won over the owners of the bellies full of beer.

"Mmmmmhhh," murmured Chrissie, "I could murder a poke o' chips right now," she said, already tasting the Dundee delicacy. "Well, we left before the pies were dished out," said Maisie, also hungry "so I think a white pudding as well wouldn't go amiss."

The pals wormed their way to the front of the queue and shouted out their order. "Make that a double," said a voice behind Maisie. Rab Skelly winked at Chrissie, "you two left in a bit of a hurry," he said, knowing exactly why they had made their quick exit. "Did you not enjoy yourselves?"

Maisie ignored him, but Chrissie didn't. "What's it to you whether we enjoyed ourselves, you and your mate didn't exactly make our night."

Rab suddenly found his blue suede shoes very interesting.

"Sorry about that," he coughed, turning to Maisie, "and Kenny's sorry as well."

At the mention of his name, Maisie instantly relived her fashion nightmare.

"A puddin' supper and a poke o' chips," said the cook, interrupting her unhappy thoughts, "that'll be two bob."

"Sorry," Maisie muttered, producing a half crown from her purse and passing the hot food to Chrissie to hold.

The girls nudged past Rab. "Tell your mate," said Maisie, regaining some of her composure, "he can keep his 'sorry' for some other mug and see this white pudding," she added, holding up the battered sausage, "this is far more interesting than he'll ever be."

"But Chrissie" Rab called after them, "what about you and me?"

Chrissie glanced over her shoulder, "there is no you and me and you can put that in your pipe and smoke it."

"There's our bus," yelled Maisie, as the Fintry bus turned up Reform Street, "Run." They jumped on the bus and scuttled up to the top deck, clutching their chips tightly till they sat down. "Whew, that was close," said Maisie, taking a bite out of her white pudding before offering a chunk to Chrissie. "That's to say thanks," she said warmly, "for standing by me."

Chrissie beamed, "it's what pals are for," she said, wisely, "and anyway, Rab Skelly's not much o' a catch anyway."

The bus lurched its way down Forfar Road to Fintry as the girls ate in comfortable silence. As they alighted, licking the last of the salt and vinegar flavoured grease from their fingers, Maisie said, "There's a Jive night at the Empress next Tuesday, maybe there'll be some half-decent lads there, if you fancy it."

"Sounds good to me," said Chrissie, "but don't mention it to my mum, I've heard it's full of old sailors looking for a 'good time' with Dundee lassies, if you get my drift."

Maisie got her drift, but in her naivety, took no notice of the warning.

"Don't be daft," she said, "old sailors can't jive."

But Maisie hadn't counted on young sailors, who could jive.

-----oOo-----

Chapter 4

The Empress Ballroom was popular with Dundee's rock and rollers, but this Tuesday there was a longer queue than usual at the door to get in. Maisie and Chrissie joined the line. "Is there something' we don't know?" asked Chrissie of the girl ahead of them.

"A tropically-tanned face with heavily made up eyes turned around. "Merchant Navy's out on strike," she stated, cracking her chewing gum seductively, "the boats are going nowhere till they get more money, so the boys are stuck in Dundee," she added grinning and leaning out to look around the queue for a likely jiving partner.

Maisie and Chrissie locked eyes, all thoughts of sailors 'on the make' dismissed, as they neared the entrance. Tonight could be the night that love sailed into their lives and Kenny and Rab could take a long walk of a short pier as far the girls were concerned, tonight they had other fish to fry.

The ballroom was electric with excitement as the jiving got under way and the glitter ball above their heads spun and sparkled. Maisie and Chrissie took to the floor, Chrissie led, as she was bigger, turning Maisie round and round, always careful not to knock the carefully coiffed beehive off its centre of balance, while the music swirled all around them.

The Green Years

"I think we're about to be tipped off," Chrissie shouted above the noise as two lads made their way onto the dance floor and headed in their direction.

"Mind if we cut in?" said the blonde Adonis to Maisie, deftly separating her from Chrissie. Maisie watched as her pal was whisked into the centre of the floor and expertly 'birrled' away. "Looks like you already have," Maisie said coyly, eyeing up the newcomer. He was a cracker, she thought to herself, not like the lads who worked at Keiller's and definitely not like Kenny Wilson. This one wasn't a teddy boy, had a proper haircut and those blue eyes! Maisie felt her knees weaken. The music stopped, signalling the end of the set and Maisie went to leave the floor, but the arm of 'blue eyes' still held her firmly around the waist as he guided her off to the side of the dance floor and the seats around the wall.

His eyes never left Maisie's face. "You've got to be the loveliest girl here," he said in a posh accent.

Maisie gasped. "Are you ENGLISH?"

Adonis smiled. "Bristol," he said, "on strike and far from home."

Maisie had never met anyone from that far away before and felt like she was discovering a new world.

"England," she breathed, "I've never met an Englishman before."

"Well, you're meeting one now," came the confident reply, "and by the way, my name's Jack, able seaman Jack Carter that is, Merchant Navy and crewman on the SS Stalwart."

Maisie was entranced. "I'm Maisie," she said shyly, I work in Keiller's and so does my friend."

"Keiller's?"

Maisie blushed, "it's a sweetie factory," she added, conscious of her Scottish accent. "Do you know what sweeties are?" she asked, immediately regretting her daftness.

Jack Carter grinned. "I think I get the picture," he said, "and you're the sweetest sweetie I've met in a long time."

The music began to slow and the lights dimmed as Fats Domino singing 'On Blueberry Hill' filled the air.

Jack took Maisie's hand. "Care to?"

Maisie felt herself being led onto the floor, then two strong arms enfolded her, pressing her against him, as the music and heat took over. All else was forgotten, as Jack kissed her neck and whispered 'sweet nothings' in her ear.

As the song ended, Jack's voice like golden syrup asked if she was hot.

Maisie nodded. "A bit," she said, hoarsely, "I could murder a coke."

"Never mind a coke," Jack said, guiding her again off the dance floor, but this time towards a fire exit, which had been opened to let in some air. "Let's go outside," he urged, "cool off a bit."

Before she knew what had happened, Maisie found herself outside in the darkness of the night, the only sound being the creak of the ships anchored nearby and the crunch of gravel beneath her feet.

Maisie felt herself shiver. "It's too cold out here," she heard herself say, "let's go back in?" But Jack Carter had been at sea a long time, and wasn't in the mood for 'going back in.'

"I'll keep you warm," he whispered, "just relax and let go."

Maisie felt his mouth on hers, hot and urgent and panic began to rise in her gut. She tried to push him away, but his iron grip stopped any escape.

"C'mon sweetie," he said, his voice turning from golden syrup to hot burnt sugar, "just feel this." He grasped

The Green Years

Maisie's wrist and forced her hand towards his crotch. "This is all for you."

All the warnings about sailors and what they were looking for flooded Maisie's young mind as a scream forced its way from her lips.

A rough hand covered her mouth. "Shut up you silly Scottish bitch," the sailor said, "you'll get me arrested."

Maisie was pushed away as the Adonis melted into the darkness. She felt tears of hurt and fear burn down her young face. She could still hear the ships creak and the waves softly lap against the harbour wall, music and laughter from the dance hall drifted into her ears, the stars shone in the night sky and stillness was everywhere.

But for Maisie Green, life would never be the same again. She had learned, the hard way, that not everyone was as they seemed to be, especially not men and definitely not sailors. On wobbly legs she slipped back into the dance hall, wondering for the first time since her encounter with Jack Carter, where Chrissie was and if she too had been tricked.

But Chrissie was safe, jiving with Jack Carter's mate and having a whale of a time. She signalled her presence when the music stopped and the 'last dance' was announced.

"See you later," Maisie mouthed, glad that at least one of them had enjoyed the night, "on the bus."

Maisie got her coat and climbed aboard the night bus, one of a number of buses laid on by the Corporation to take late revellers home to the housing schemes.

She still felt shaken by her experience outside the dance hall and lit a cigarette, drawing heavily on the tobacco to calm her down.

She heard Chrissie giggling before she saw her. Her best friend in the whole world was closely followed by a tousle-haired, sweating young man, who seemed to be unable to stop grinning.

"Maisie," Chrissie cried, "where did you disappear to?" she asked with a knowing smile, plonking herself down in the seat in front of Maisie, with her escort parking himself alongside her.

Maisie sat grim-faced and tight lipped.

"What's the matter?" asked Chrissie, nudging the man to also turn round to face Maisie.

The smile faded from the young man's face.

"Has Jack Carter been up to no good again?" he asked.

Maisie felt tears beginning to reform in her eyes.

"Again?" she managed to ask.

Chrissie looked puzzled. "Up to what, Tommy?" she asked.

"I know he's a mate of mine," Tommy said, "but I'm afraid he's no respecter of women."

Maisie felt sick. How could she have been so naive and trusting? How could she have been so stupid as not to see what Jack Carter was really after?

Chrissie pushed past Tommy and took her place beside Maisie.

"Oh, Maisie," she whispered, taking her hand. "Whatever it is, it'll be alright. Tommy'll make sure we both get home safely," she said, "won't you Tommy?" He nodded, "and when I get back to the ship, I'll make sure he knows what a bastard he is."

Even the word shocked Maisie. From feeling very grown up on becoming runner-up in the Miss Keiller's beauty contest, she now felt like a lost five year old with a lot to learn.

-----oOo-----

Chapter 5

Next day, at work, Maisie appeared the same, but underneath she knew things were different. The trust she had had in her world and the people around her had taken a knock and been replaced by fear and uncertainty. Jack Carter had seemed so clean cut, so much a gentleman and all her instincts had been to trust him. How wrong she had been and it had shaken her confidence more than she cared to admit.

She was still in this state of introspection as she sat at one of the canteen tables with her bacon roll and mug of tea.

"Mind if I join you," asked the male voice, sliding his tray onto the table and pulling up a chair. Maisie looked up and into the eyes of Kenny Wilson.

"Yes, I do mind," Maisie told him, snappily, "I'd prefer to be alone."

Kenny raised his eyebrows in disbelief. Maisie Green was telling him to buzz off!

"No need to be like that Maisie," he said, smarting from her rejection of his company, "I just wanted to say...."

"There's nothing you can say that I want to hear," Maisie countered loudly, before he could say anymore. "So just GO, alright!" she added angrily.

Fellow workers round about them began to nudge one another, with the women especially interested at Kenny Wilson seeming to be given the 'BIG E.'

"You tell him Maisie," shouted Betty Morrison, particularly pleased at the altercation, as she was one of Kenny's 'rejects' herself.

Kenny felt his face burn with embarrassment and humiliation, but remained in his seat. No woman was going to tell him what to do.

"I'm not for leaving Maisie Green," he said slowly, leaning forward, "but if you want to bugger off, then ta ta." He waved a hand in front of Maisie's face.

Maisie's bravado faded. For the second time in a row, she'd been made a fool of by a man and as the last of her confidence evaporated in tearful confusion, she ran from the canteen to the cheers of the men and the silence of the women.

Blinded by tears, she hurried to the Ladies, only to be stopped in her tracks by the bulk of Rab Skelly.

"Hey, hey," he said, holding onto Maisie's shoulders, "where's the fire?"

Maisie tried to push him away, but the fight had gone out of her.

"Ask your pal," she whispered, bitterly, "and tell him from me to go to Hell."

Rab frowned and released his grip, watching Maisie's back till she disappeared into the women's toilets.

What had Kenny done now, he wondered, as he headed to the canteen. He thought his mate fancied Maisie, but whatever he'd said to her, clearly hadn't worked.

He found Kenny alone and staring at the half-eaten bacon roll Maisie had left.

"What's up Ken," he said cheerfully, pointing to the uneaten food, "not hungry then?"

"She just dumped me," Kenny said slowly, "and in front of everybody."

Rab looked around at the mix of workers who had turned back to the business of eating, now that the 'fun' was over.

He knew who Kenny was talking about but feigned ignorance.

"What!"

Kenny's still stunned eyes met his.

"Maisie Green," he told him, "just dumped me. ME, Kenny Wilson and in front of everybody."

Rab glanced over his shoulder. "I don't think anybody noticed Kenny," he said in a reassuring voice, "and by the state of Maisie Green in the corridor just now, it looked more like you dumped her."

Kenny brightened. "Upset was she?"

"Very!"

He pushed his chair back and looked around. Rab was right, nobody seemed bothered, too busy feeding their faces.

But Kenny was bothered. Maisie's rejection had shook him up. For the first time in his handsome life, he'd been rejected by a woman.

Chrissie came rushing into the Ladies. "Maisie!" she exclaimed, "are you OK?" Maisie sniffed and nodded. "Betty Morrison told me what happened with that swine Kenny Wilson in the canteen....."

Maisie held up her hand to silence Chrissie, as she dabbed her red swollen eyes with a wet hankie.

"Its fine Chrissie, honest," Maisie tried to assure her, "but now's not the time or place to speak about this. The Supervisor will be on our necks if we don't get back to work."

Chrissie agreed. "How about we go to Wallaces Tearoom later for a pie and beans, get this off your chest?" Chrissie blushed, remembering the 'shoulder pad' incident at Keiller's dance. "Sorry Maisie," she stammered, "didn't mean to remind you of...." Maisie shoved her gently towards the door.

"C'mon," she said, "let's get back to work."

Wallaces Tearoom was quiet, with only a few tables taken by men on their own, filling up on pies and bridies before hitting the pubs for a 'session.'

The waitress showed them to a table at the back of the tearoom where they could have 'privacy' as Maisie put it.

The order for pie and beans was placed accompanied by a large pot of tea and the two girls got down to the task of understanding men and two men in particular.

"I just don't get it!" Maisie stated bluntly "are all lads only after one thing?"

Chrissie shrugged and dipped her knife into her hot pie.

"Tommy's not," she said, a forkful of pie midway between plate and mouth, "Tommy's lovely." Chrissie chewed thoughtfully. "He's going to write to me every day he's at sea and send photos and everything."

Maisie was stunned. "But, you've only just met!" she exclaimed, "how can you tell he's....well....decent?"

"Can't," Chrissie replied, with the wisdom of her sixteen years, "but **I know** what's right and, anyway I don't intend to end up like smellie Jean, with a bairn at fifteen and no man."

Maisie sat back in her chair, her pie growing cold. "And he didn't 'try anything on' last night?"

Chrissie scooped up more beans. "Nope."

Maisie frowned, "then it must be me," she reasoned, "I must be giving off some vibes or something."

Chrissie poured herself a cup of tea. "Are you not hungry?" she asked, pointing to the untouched pie and beans. Maisie pushed the plate towards her friend, "help yourself," she said, "I couldn't eat a thing."

Chrissie sighed, usually it was she who bemoaned her *lack of attention* from boys and for the first time, felt sorry for Maisie and her good looks. "So you've had a bit of bad luck with the laddies," she counselled, "but you're a bonnie lassie Maisie and if you don't want lads to fancy you, then you'd better stop being a wee smasher or get really good at saying **NO**."

Maisie smiled at her friend's black and white answer.

"So, that's it," she said, "just say NO!"

"That's it," said Chrissie, "and don't go out the back of dance halls with wandering sailors either!"

Maisie relaxed. Chrissie was right. The choice was hers about 'how far to go' with a lad and until she fell in love, she decided, really fell in love, her answer would always be NO.

She pulled the plate of pie and beans over to her side of the table. "I think I've got my appetite back," she said, picking up her knife and fork, "and Kenny Wilson had better watch out."

-----oOo-----

Chapter 6

"I'm bored," announced Maisie to her mother one Sunday, who was busying herself, as usual, in the kitchen. It had been a few weeks now since her encounter with Jack Carter but the memory still played on her mind. Her mother ignored her.

"There's nothing to do on a Sunday," she bemoaned sighing deeply, and gazing out of the window at the drying green with its patch of daisy-strewn grass.

Her mother stopped her dish washing and looked at her daughter, even without makeup and her hair tousled around her face, she was pretty. Didn't she realise how lucky she was, carefree and single and not burdened down with a sick husband and a shortage of money. The young nowadays, she tutted to herself, don't know they're born. She turned back to the dishes.

"Away and get out in the fresh air," she said, dismissively. Her daughter was right, there was nothing to do on Sunday in Dundee, as everything was closed for the 'day of rest' with the churches being the only option available and not everyone was drawn to their preaching of 'doom and gloom'.

"Or you could clean your room, or cut the grass, or help me with the dishes....." Maisie covered her ears, "alright," she said, loudly, not wanting to hear any more of her mother's suggestions, "I'll get some fresh air."

The Green Years

Slipping on her flat shoes and a big 'cardie', she headed off to Chrissie's. She needed company and cheering up after her recent 'man troubles' and maybe her mother was right, a walk in the fresh air might just lift her spirits.

"Go for a walk!" Chrissie exclaimed, rubbing her sleepy eyes when she heard Maisie's Sunday suggestion. "Walk where?"

Maisie shrugged. How about the Den o' Mains?" she suggested, "it's no' far and the sun's shining.................a bit!"

"Give's a mo'," Chrissie replied, reluctantly, nodding her ascent and leaving Maisie standing on the doorstep.

A minute later she was back, a pair of 'wellies' on her feet and a duffle coat pegged shut across her chest.

Maisie tried not to giggle. "You're not going out like that......"

she began, then realised that Chrissie would be going nowhere if she didn't shut up.

"Sorry," she said, anxiously, indicating her error of judgement, "perfect walking gear."

The two friends set off, leaving Fintry behind and crossing Forfar Road into the vale that was the Den o' Mains. Following the stream that ran though the dip between the two steep grassy slopes either side, they made their way to the ponds that fed the stream and sat down on a bench in the leafy quietness.

A few dog walkers passed by, nodding 'hello' as they went and a pair of young lads, with fishing nets and jam jars, were trawling the pond for minnows and tadpoles, but apart from that, all was peaceful. The rays of a weak September sun strengthened and Chrissie untoggled her heavy coat and wished she'd worn her old sandshoes. The 'wellies' were making her feet sweat.

"Isn't it lovely here," Maisie whispered, feeling the sun and silence soaking into her body.

Chrissie gave her a quizzical look, "It's the Den o' Mains," she said, slowly, "not the Costa Brava."

Maisie shrugged. "I know," she said, "I just wish I could meet someone really special and get married and everything before I get too old."

"You're sixteen!"

Maisie turned to her friend, "I'll be seventeen in December," she reminded her, "and the way things have been going lately, I don't think I'll ever meet Mr Right. What if I die an 'auld maid'?"

Chrissie fell silent. She'd received another letter from Tommy Murphy, posted from Gibraltar, pledging undying love and enclosing a photo of himself. He'd been at sea a month now and he'd written every week, but she hadn't yet told Maisie about the correspondence, not wanting to remind her of Jack Carter and what he did.

"Maybe we should go to the 'Monkey Parade' tonight," Chrissie suggested, trying to lighten Maisie's introspective mood, "see if there's any 'talent' around."

Due to the lack of anything interesting to do on Sunday, the young and single had taken to walking up and down the Murraygate in the early evening, finally ending up at the 'Palais de Dance Ballroom, where the walking continued, at the cost of 1/- entry fee and no dancing, drinking or 'hanky panky' allowed, just walking round and round the dance floor, eyeing up the talent. Of course, there was always a chance of seeing someone you 'fancied' and which could be followed up at a later date, if you were lucky.

"Mmmmm," said Maisie, brightening up a bit, "no point in crying over spilt milk I suppose" she added, "and I don't think my 'knight in shining armour' is going to turn up here, is he?" she shrugged, looking dismally around her.

But unknown to them, Maisie and Chrissie were being watched. Two young men had been drinking beer amongst the shrubbery on the other side of the pond, and as their alcohol intake rose, so did their courage.

"Which one do you fancy Ronnie?"

Ronnie Reid grinned. "Not the one with the 'wellies'" he replied, smirking, "you can have her, I'm for the other one."

His brother Johnny sniffed. "Maybe, she'll no fancy you," he mumbled.

"That's never going to happen," said Ronnie, confidently, knocking back the last of his can of beer and brushing the grass from his jeans, "c'mon."

The two lads broke cover just a Maisie and Chrissie began to make their way back down towards the open valley below.

"Going our way?" Ronnie called to their backs.

The girls turned, taking in the two men, leather jackets clinking with chains and black biker boots laced over black jeans.

Maisie nudged Chrissie. "Let's get moving" she whispered, not liking what she saw and aware that even the two young fishermen had vanished. They were alone.

Chrissie linked her arm into Maisie's as they quickened their walk, but a strong hand gripped Maisie's arm.

"What's the hurry, girls?" he said turning Maisie towards him.

Maisie could smell the drink on his breath and shook her arm free.

"No hurry," she said, faking a bravado she didn't feel.

"So just beetle off, we're busy O.K.

"No need to be like that hen," he retorted, "me an' the brother were just admirin' two bonnie lassies, that's all!" He raised his shoulders and spread his arms, "that no right Johnny?" he asked his brother, who was now blocking any further progress down the path.

"Right enough," Johnny agreed, fingering the toggle on Chrissie's coat.

Chrissie slapped his hand away, "Get off me," she said loudly, "and out o' my way." The two girls made to push free but they were no match for the brothers. Maisie felt panic rising in her throat. This was 'Jack Carter' all over again! She began to struggle and tears blurred her eyes as she felt Ronnie Reid's hand find its way under her cardigan. Suddenly, the sound of a dog barking and the deep voice of a man met her ears.

"HEY, YOU TWO," the voice shouted, "FUCK OFF **NOW** OR I'LL SET THE DOG ON THE PAIR OF YOU." Maisie felt herself being pushed roughly into the bushes and could hear footsteps running away. Chrissie was beside her in a heap, her face scarlet and a toggle missing from her duffle coat.

"Are you lassies alright?" asked the dog owner anxiously, helping them to their feet.

"We're fine," Maisie nodded shakily, "they came from nowhere," she added, trying to explain. "We were just heading home when they came up behind us......"

Maisie was taking deep breaths trying to calm down and Chrissie was still too shaken to move. Irrationally, she was trying to understand how she'd explain the missing toggle to her mother.

"Do you live nearby, asked their rescuer?

Maisie indicated Fintry. "C'mon then," came the reply, "me and the dog'll see you both safely home."

The liquid brown eyes of the Alsatian dog watched the scene. He'd never know his role in the rescue, but Maisie would never forget him or, for that matter, his master.

When they got back to the safety of Fintry and 'civilisation,' Ian Brown introduced himself. "And this is Rebel," he said, proudly. "Now, shake hands with the nice ladies," he instructed the dog who duly stretched out a paw for the girls to shake.

"We can't thank you enough," Maisie said, "and Rebel," she added, truly grateful.

"No bother," said Ian Brown, his eyes locking on to Maisie's "maybe I'll see you around sometime."

"Maybe," Maisie replied, sensing something a bit different about the man with the dog called Rebel.

"Well," said Chrissie, after Ian Brown had gone, "next time you want to get some fresh air, count me OUT."

Maisie agreed. "Is there nowhere safe" she wondered aloud?

"Doesn't look like it," Chrissie said, linking into Maisie again.

"How about coming to us for Sunday tea," she added, "mum's making her famous Shepherd's Pie and Apple Tart with custard?"

"How can I refuse," Maisie replied, a smile beginning to return to her lips, "but only if you're sure there'll be enough?"

Chrissie tutted, "have you ever known my mother not making enough to feed a regiment?"

Chrissie's mother, Grace, was the most generous woman Maisie had ever met. Her door was always open and her cooker never without something boiling or stewing away on it. And if laughter was something you could order, Grace Dalton had it in bucket loads.

A seat at her table was just what Maisie needed to cheer her up and to wipe out the memory of the louts in the Den o' Mains.

"Let's go then," she said, "Your mum's Shepherd's Pie is just what I need."

-----oOo-----

Chapter 7

Any thoughts of going to the Monkey Parade later that Sunday were discarded, both girls just wanting a quiet night in to recover from their ordeal.

"Any idea who they were?" asked Chrissie, after they'd polished off their meal and adjourned to her bedroom for a ciggie.

Maisie shook her head. "Not a clue," she said, "and I never want to see either of them again." She rolled onto her back and gazed at the ceiling, "is there not a man out there we can trust Chrissie, I mean really believe in?"

"I've something to tell you," Chrissie suddenly announced, rummaging through the drawer of her bedside table and producing a small handful of cream coloured envelopes.

She'd been hoping for an opportunity to tell Maisie all about Tommy Murphy, but none had arisen so she decided now was as good a time as any to spill the beans.

"Do you remember the sailor who took us home that night from the Empress, Tommy Murphy?"

Maisie nodded, her lips tightening as she again remembered Jack Carter's unwanted advances.

"What about him?"

Chrissie handed her friend the bundle of envelopes. "Well, he's been writing to me for weeks now and he says he loves me."

Maisie turned the envelopes over in her hand in silence.

Sensing the change in atmosphere, Chrissie hurried on, "I didn't like to mention him before, in case it got you upset, with that Jack Carter an' all, but we seem to be getting on really well and....."

Maisie held up her hand. "It's OK," she said, quietly, "I understand. I just wish I could meet someone," she sighed, feeling more alone than ever "and be able to trust them like you have, but everyone I meet turns out to be a bad lot."

First, there was the hideous Shug Reilly, peering down her frock at Keiller's dance, then the smug Kenny Wilson who had laughed at her embarrassment on the dance floor. But worst of all, Jack Carter, who she had felt could have been 'the one' but who had made her totally doubt herself and her judgement of men.

The two 'chancers' at the Den 'o Mains were at least obvious, Maisie thought, not pretending to be something they weren't.

She shivered at the memory of the close encounter and, once more, felt grateful to Rebel and Ian Brown for their rescue.

Chrissie had been feeling a bit guilty about keeping secrets from her very best friend and was glad Tommy Murphy was now out in the open.

"C'mon," said Maisie, "let's have one more cig then I'll be off home to bed. Work tomorrow," she added, relieved that the day was almost over and tomorrow would bring back some normality into her life.

The sweet aroma of butterscotch and chocolate filled the air as the two girls 'clocked on' at Keiller's on Monday morning and headed to the Packing Department. The noise of chattering females and metal trays of chocolates being delivered to their tables for packing, kept any

Sandra Savage

conversation to a minimum and it was as Maisie and Chrissie were heading for the canteen, it happened.

Maisie felt something hard hit her head and bounce off again, landing at her feet. Rubbing her head, she looked down to the floor, a butterscotch sweet wrapped in its golden paper lay at her feet. She picked it up. Written on the paper in very small print were the words 'look up.'

Maisie and Chrissie looked up simultaneously and there, on top of a stack of wooden pallets were Kenny Wilson and Rab Skelly.

"Hi girls," Rab called, grinning, "remember us?"

Maisie frowned. What was Kenny Wilson up to? She thought she'd made it perfectly clear that she wanted nothing more to do with him!

Both girls shrugged and after directing a scathing look at the lads, moved off.

"Well, that went well," said Kenny, sarcastically, any more brilliant ideas?"

"Chrissie gave me a dirty look as well," he huffed, "it's not just you that's been dumped."

Kenny felt his stomach tense. "I've not been dumped," he announced, angrily, "it was me that dumped her......remember?"

"Then," Rab bristled, "why are you so keen to get Maisie's attention then?"

"Simple," came the reply, "'cause NOBODY makes a fool of ME and if it's the last thing I do it'll be to get the better of Maisie Green."

Rab raised his eyebrows. "Oh, yeah," he retorted, "and how does that work then?"

"It works," replied Kenny, warming to his topic, "when Miss Green agrees to go out with me and........well, does the term 'Duffers Corner' mean anything to you?"

"You mean?"

The Green Years

Kenny smiled and tightened his belt a notch. "The lovely lady is going to find out the hard way, that you don't mess with the big boys and get off with it."

He slapped Rab on the back, "C'mon," he said, "we've got work to do."

"What was all that about?" Chrissie asked, as the girls made their way back to their work tables.

"I was wondering that as well," Maisie replied, "if it wasn't so ridiculous, I'd think they were trying to get our attention."

"Why is it ridiculous Maisie?"

"Do I have to remind you of Keiller's dance?" Maisie queried.

Chrissie frowned. "Maybe Kenny's sorry, or something'"

"Huh!"

Chrissie shrugged her shoulders. "Well, I've got Tommy," she reminded Maisie, wistfully, "so Rab Skelly can just get lost."

The girls bent to their task of chocolate packing, but Maisie was confused. Could it possibly be that Kenny Wilson was sorry, really sorry! She considered her options. Go on ignoring him, let him worry about her feelings for a change, or accept his apology, if that was what this was all about.......she made up her mind and focussed her attention back on the job. Ignoring him, her ego decided, felt great.

The rest of the week went by without any further approaches by Kenny, but Maisie never missed an opportunity to sweep past him in the canteen, avoiding all eye contact, as she chattered and giggled with the other girls in the tea queue.

"She doesn't seem to be bothered Kenny?" said Rab, watching Maisie over the rim of his mug on the Friday afternoon,

"It's an act," came the sharp reply.

"Quite the wee actress then," Rab countered, now quite enjoying Kenny' discomfort. He was Kenny's best mate, but there were times when he found his super confidence a bit annoying, especially with women.

Kenny returned his mug to the table and stood up as Maisie headed towards the canteen door. "Follow me."

The two lads caught up with Maisie as she turned into the corridor.

"Maisie," Kenny called out, "wait up."

Maisie turned, her defences primed and at the ready. Here was the apology that she had coming, she told herself. It was time for Kenny Wilson to grovel.

"Well," she said, primly, "what do you two want?"

Rab stepped back, his hands raised in surrender.

"Nothin' Maisie," he said, "it's just Kenny wants a word."

Maisie's eyes levelled with her enemy. His brown eyes were liquid with sorrow as his hand ran anxiously through the waves of dark hair falling onto his brow.

Maisie felt her knees go weak and her steely resolve soften slightly "Have you got a minute, Maisie?" he asked, his voice taking on a slight tremor of emotion.

Maisie nodded. She suddenly had a lifetime of minutes for Kenny Wilson.

He stretched out one arm and braced his hand against the wall at the side of Maisie, placing the other hand on his hip while contemplating the floor for 'inspiration.'

Rab was mesmerised. Kenny was masterful.

"Are you ever going to speak to me again?" he whispered, still keeping his eyes on his feet.

Maisie felt her throat constrict.

"Maybe!" she said, hoarsely.

Kenny felt his confidence rise. Now he'd go in for the kill.

The Green Years

"Then how about," he raised his eyes to meet hers, "me and you giving it another go?"

Maisie felt the last of her resolve vanish. Maybe Kenny wasn't exactly apologising, but he felt really sorry for laughing at her, she was sure of that.

Maisie nodded, "OK," she replied, "if you like."

Kenny placed his hand on her shoulder and squeezed it gently.

"I'll get back to you on that one Maisie," he smarmed, "soon, very soon."

With those words, he turned to Rab. "Palais tonight?" he said. Rab nodded in complete awe of Kenny Wilson's power over women, "and who knows," he turned back to Maisie, "maybe the girl of my dreams will turn up there as well."

Maisie stood perfectly still as she watched the back of Kenny Wilson disappear down the corridor. Was that a suggestion, or an invitation, or a heavy date! Maisie had to find Chrissie, and quick. They had to get organised for going dancing tonight at the Palais de Dance. The girl of Kenny's dreams was going to be her.

-----oOo-----

Chapter 8

When Maisie finally got her legs to move again, she hurried back to her work table. "Chrissie," she hissed, motioning her friend to follow her to the Ladies.

Chrissie looked round, Mrs Hutchieson, the Supervisor was deep in conversation with the Bonus Checker, Ella Smart. She nodded to Maisie and quietly sidled towards the door and out into the corridor.

Maisie was pacing up and down the toilet floor with excitement.

"What's up?"

Maisie pulled her friend to the far end of the toilets and lowered her voice.

"Kenny Wilson's just spoken to me," she said, "and we've to meet him and Rab at the Palais tonight."

Chrissie's mouth fell open in shock. "But, you said......"

Maisie hushed her up. "I know what I said, but that was last week, it's different now."

Chrissie felt more confused, till Maisie related the encounter with Kenny, word for word. "So, you see," she ended, "we just have to be there."

"Are you sure, this is what you want?" Chrissie asked, concerned at Maisie's total change of heart. "You're not rushing into things again are you?"

Maisie placed her hands on her hips, slightly chastened by Chrissie's comment. She didn't rush into things did she?

The Green Years

And Kenny had been so sincere, how could she possibly doubt him.

"No," she said firmly. "Now, are we going tonight or not?"

Chrissie pushed down the unease that had formed at Maisie's news. Leopards don't change their spots, she believed, and Kenny Wilson was indisputably the 'spottiest leopard in the jungle.'

"OK," Chrissie sighed, "if you're really sure."

Maisie hugged her friend.

"You're the best Chrissie Dalton," she said, "I'll see you at seven, my place."

The date agreed, the two girls hurried back to finish their shift.

The Supervisor was always on the look-out for slackers and neither of them could afford to be sacked.

"See you at seven," Maisie mouthed as they made their way back to their work tables. Tonight was going to be wonderful, she told herself, all the feelings she'd had for Kenny now enveloped her again, and this time, even stronger.

Maybe it had taken kissing a few frogs before finally meeting her Prince Charming, but it was all worth it now. Kenny would be hers, at last.

The Palais was packed with dancers of all ages, all dressed to thrill and looking for 'real' love. The lads swaggered around the dance hall, taking sly nips from quarter bottles of whisky concealed in their jackets, while the girls danced with one another, pretending not to notice them.

"Any sign of them yet?" Maisie was looking anxiously around Chrissie while trying to keep up with the fast paced jive in the black stilettos she still hadn't returned to her friend.

Maisie twirled Chrissie till she was facing the doors. It was past nine o'clock and the pubs would be chucking out soon, so where was Kenny? Surely, he wasn't going to turn up drunk!

The music stopped and Chrissie suggested they get themselves a cold drink in the cafe downstairs. Chrissie nodded and followed her, all the while, glancing over her shoulder in the hope that Kenny would suddenly appear.

"It's a wee while till closing time," Chrissie said, pushing a bottle of ice-cold coco-cola towards Maisie, "he'll turn up soon."

But Maisie wasn't so sure. She relived the moment of their earlier encounter. "He definitely said, he'd be at the Palais to meet 'the girl of his dreams' and that definitely meant ME."

The girls fell into a confused silence.

"Mind if I join you?" asked a man, pulling up a chair from another table. "How have you both been?"

Maisie turned to face the owner of the voice. He did look familiar, but in the low lights of the cafeteria, she couldn't be sure. "Do we know you?" she asked, her eyes squinting into his. "It's Ian," he said, "Ian Brown."

"Rebel's dad?" Maisie asked incredulously.

Ian laughed. "Well, I'm not his dad exactly, more his master, but yep, that's me."

"But, you look so different!" Maisie exclaimed, taking in the dark suit and white shirt and tie, I didn't recognise you."

She turned to Chrissie for confirmation, "did you know who he was?" But Chrissie was already on her feet, draining the last few drops of her 'coke' through the straw. "Sure," she said, "nice to see you again. But if you don't mind, I need to visit the Ladies."

Maisie watched as Chrissie left the two of them at the table, with a wave and a knowing smile.

The Green Years

Maybe Maisie hadn't spotted it, but Chrissie had, Ian Brown had 'the hots' for Maisie.

"So," he began, with a laugh, "do you come here often?"

Maisie acknowledged the corny line and sipped her drink, careful to avoid any slurping sounds.

Ian offered her a cigarette. "No boyfriend then?"

Maisie put down the coke and allowed him to light the filter tipped cigarette. "Not at the moment," she said, realising for a minute she'd forgotten about Kenny Wilson and wondering how she'd missed the handsome Ian Brown at their first encounter.

"And you," she asked, "I mean, no girlfriend?"

Ian shook his head. "There's just me and Rebel and work."

He pulled his chair in closer and leaned forward.

"Are you for a dance, when you've finished your drink?"

Maisie was about to answer when she saw the frantic figure of Chrissie waving and pointing up the stairs while mouthing the words KENNY WILSON.

He was here and Maisie's world was about to burst into wonderfulness. She looked at Ian Brown.

"Sorry," she said, abruptly, standing up and moving away from the table, "not tonight."

She hurried over to Chrissie, leaving Ian Brown in her wake.

"He's here Maisie," Chrissie whispered, "but he's, kind of DRUNK." Maisie winced in disbelief.

"Over there," Chrissie pointed, "and I think he's seen us!"

Kenny Wilson had indeed seen them, and after nudging Rab to follow him, made his way unsteadily towards them.

The smell of alcohol almost knocked Maisie backwards, as Kenny pulled her towards the dance floor.

"Been waiting long?" he slurred.

Maisie cringed. So, this was how Kenny Wilson treated the 'girl of his dreams.'

Angrily, Maisie pushed him away and walked off the floor. How could he, she fumed, realising it had all been an act. She wasn't the girl of his dreams at all, just another notch on his conceited belt.

"C'mon Chrissie," she said, vowing never to let any man fool her again, "let's go." She drew a glance at Rab Skelly. "And, as for you," she murmured, "time you grew up."

"But, Maisie," Rab protested, "it wasn't my fault he got drunk. I'm not his keeper."

"Well you should be," interrupted Chrissie, "because the man's an ANIMAL."

Maisie and Chrissie headed to the cloakroom for their coats.

"Are you alright Maisie?" Chrissie asked gently. She knew how much this night had meant to her pal and, now, it had ended in heartbreak for her again. She was glad that she had Tommy Murphy to love, even if it was on paper, but he'd be back in Dundee soon when his ship docked for repairs and then she'd know for sure, if he really, really, did love her like he'd said in his letters.

The girls left the dance hall and merged into the darkness of a cold Scottish night. The walk to their bus stop would be a chilly one after the heat of the dance hall, but as they hurried away their departure was being watched from the doorway by Ian Brown. He'd seen it all, and when the bouncers had chucked the two drunks out, he'd realised that if that was who Maisie had left him at the table for, then he had a chance with her and, somehow, he'd find a way to get close to her again.

He lit a cigarette and walked to his car, parked in the Nethergate. Rebel whined at his approach, his tail now wagging as Ian opened the car door and clipped on his lead.

The Green Years

He'd take a walk down by Magdalen Green, let Rebel off the lead for a bit, before reporting for duty at the NCR.

Security Dog Handler, Ian Brown liked the night shift. Between patrolling the factory grounds and checking everything was securely locked at the National Cash Register Company, he had plenty of time to think about life, and Ian thought a lot. But, tonight he would be thinking about one thing only and that would be how to win the heart of Maisie Green.

-----oOo-----

Chapter 9

The bus ride home was taken in silence, Chrissie lost in thoughts of Tommy Murphy and Maisie tired and angry with herself and the drunken Kenny Wilson. He was certainly giving her mixed messages and, at sixteen, she was having great difficulty translating the 'code of love.'

She felt it was no longer a case of 'just saying NO,' it was more like who to say YES to? Everybody around Maisie seemed to be 'in the know' when it came to affairs of the heart. She'd seen couples everywhere, smiling and holding hands as they strolled through life, but for her, it seemed more like an uphill struggle than a stroll!

Then, there was her mum and dad. Was this what love was all about? Nearly every night, they sat watching the telly till it was bedtime, never speaking much, except to share a last cup of tea and biscuit before turning in. Was that her future too?

Chrissie's nudge broke into her thoughts. "C'mon," she said, "it's our stop." The girls alighted into the cold and darkness. "See you later," Chrissie's sleepy voice whispered.

Maisie blinked, "Yeah," she said woodenly, "later."

Chrissie hesitated, but couldn't think of anything helpful to say, as Maisie walked off towards home, her head filled with thoughts of what she wanted her life to be like and not what it was turning out to be.

The Green Years

She had dreams of 'knights in shining armour' crossing the burning desert to rescue her, or being swept off her feet by a handsome suitor, bold and brave and ready to lay down his life to protect her.

She turned into the garden gate and looked around her into the dimness of the street. But, what had she really got, the attention of a drunken Kenny Wilson and a job as a chocolate packer in a sweetie factory. Maisie sighed. Right now, she wished she was anyone but Maisie Green.

"You're early," her mother's voice called out when Maisie looked into the living room. She took in the scene, same as usual, TV switched on, lives switched off.

"Make your dad and me a cuppa will you, before you go to bed, my bunions are giving me jip."

Maisie smiled sadly, "sure thing mum," she said, "and a bicci?"

Mrs Green nodded, her eyes never leaving the television set.

Maisie set about the task, she loved her mum and dad, but she was determined that their fate, wouldn't be hers. Something had to change and it was up to Maisie to make it change. She didn't quite know how she was going to do this, but somehow, she felt certain she would.

She'd talk things over with Chrissie tomorrow. Maybe she knew the answer, maybe not, but for now, she would make tea for all three of them, then sleep on it and forget all about tonight.

Despite everything, Maisie slept well and woke with a determined resolve that her life must change. She looked around the small bedroom, with its faded wallpaper and linoleum floor covering. The lampshade in the centre of the ceiling, with its tired fringe, looked back. Her bed was alright, she decided, but the pink candlewick bedspread had seen better days and as for the basket chair in the corner, where she usually kept her pyjamas, it was only fit for the bin. She threw back the bedclothes and pushed her feet into her woolly slippers.

After breakfast, she'd make a plan. Yes, that's what she'd do, make a plan to first change her bedroom and then change her life. Maisie felt a rush of energy, at last she was taking control of her future and it was going to be wonderful. And it didn't include Kenny Wilson.

She could smell bacon frying and her appetite sharpened, nothing like a bacon roll to get your taste buds wakened up.

Esther Green was cutting and spreading the Aberdeen Butteries when her daughter came into the kitchen.

"Morning mum," she beamed, "Can I have an egg roll as well as a bacon one?"

Her mother eyed her warily, "you seem bright and breezy for a Saturday morning'" she said, "that early night's done you some good then?"

Mrs Green cracked an egg into the hot fat, before placing the bacon roll in front of her daughter and pouring her a cup of tea.

She sensed something had changed in her daughter, but for the life of her she couldn't think what.

"I've been wondering," Maisie began, as her mother flipped the fried egg over before tipping it onto another roll and adding it to Maisie's plate.

"Oh aye," she said, a slight unease creeping into her voice, hoping against hope that Maisie wasn't going to start asking her awkward questions about men and their 'needs'.

Maisie bit into her bacon roll, it really was the best thing in the world for breakfast she decided and chewed hungrily before continuing.

"I was wondering if I could miss my board money for a couple of weeks," Maisie asked, "I was thinking of doing up my room.....sort off..."

The Green Years

Maisie's mother didn't know whether to laugh or cry. So, that was what all this new found energy was about. "You can do what you like with your room Maisie," she replied, raising her daughter's hopes, "but your board money's needed to keep the wolf from the door, so whatever you've got in mind, you'd better just forget it."

Maisie felt like a bucket of cold water had been poured over her. So much for her plan to become a new woman, she couldn't even get her plans for her revamped bedroom off the ground.

"But, it would only be for a couple o' weeks," she protested, "and I'd do it all myself......." Her mother held up a stopping palm.

"Sorry Maisie," she said, genuinely feeling remorse for the refusal, but knowing how much the weekly board money helped keep them fed, "it just can't be done."

Maisie pushed the uneaten egg roll away, once again reality had kicked her dreams into touch and her appetite seemed to have vanished with them.

Fighting back the disappointment, Maisie forced a smile. She knew only too well how little money they had to live on.

"Ne'er mind," she murmured, "it was just a thought."

She turned to go. Maybe Chrissie would have some ideas. Changing your life wasn't nearly as easy as Maisie had first thought, but failing at the first hurdle wasn't an option either, she told herself, remembering the story of Robert the Bruce and the spider. She'd keep trying she decided shakily, till someday she'd get herself the new life she wanted.

"Are you not wanting that egg roll?" her mother called out after her, keenly aware that it wouldn't go to waste.

"You have it," Maisie called back, "I've just put myself on a diet."

Sandra Savage

It was with a heavy heart that Maisie knocked on Chrissie's door later that morning. Grace Dalton opened the door and immediately knew something was wrong.

"What's to do Maisie?" she asked gently, "you look right fed up."

Maisie looked at the concerned face of Chrissie's mother. How different she was from her own mother, but then, Mrs Dalton's life was very different. Her husband had a good job in Timex and there was never a fear of hunger in her house.

How unfair everything seemed to her young mind.

"It's nothing much Mrs Dalton, just that I wanted to pretty my bedroom up a bit, but mum says we can't afford it."

Grace Dalton hustled Maisie through to the kitchen. "I'll let Chrissie know you're here in a minute," she said, "but firstly, tell me all about it and I'll see if there isn't something can be done."

She made up two glasses of orange squash for them and sat down opposite her daughter's best friend. Maisie told Grace Dalton of her plans, of how she wanted to have a better life and how she couldn't even improve her bedroom, never mind anything else.

"What sort of thing were you looking for to improve your room?" Grace asked.

Maisie tried to sound positive as she disclosed her short list of essentials, bedspread, small table and lamp, basket chair and lampshade.

Well, that doesn't sound too demanding," said Mrs Dalton, refilling Maisie's glass. "Did Chrissie tell you I was in the WI?"

Maisie shook her head. "The WI," she said, "what's that?"

"It's the Womens Institute and we're having a jumble sale at the Fintry Church Hall this Saturday. I'm running one of the stalls, so I'll get to choose what I think will sell on my table and maybe I could look out for one or two things for you."

Maisie couldn't believe her ears. "But, I don't have much money," she began. Grace Dalton laughed. "It's a jumble sale Maisie, not Draffens and we get all sorts donated. Now I'm not saying there will be anything useful for you, but I'll certainly keep my eyes open."

Maisie felt her spirits rise. So, change was possible, she realised, it was just that sometimes, you also had to have a bit of luck on your side, like knowing Chrissie and her mother.

"I'll let Chrissie know you're here," smiled Grace Dalton, glad that she might be able to do something for Maisie. She knew the Greens and Joe Green's health problems and thanked God for her own security. She was one of the lucky ones, she had a working husband. But Maisie decided she wanted to go home now and begin cleaning her bedroom.

"I'll see Chrissie tomorrow," she said, thanking Mrs Dalton, for the orange squash and for her kindness.

Grace Dalton saw her to the door. Jumble sale or not, she decided, Maisie Green was going to have what she needed to change her bedroom. As for her future, Grace pondered, maybe that too could change if, like her, she found a good man to love her.

It took Maisie the rest of Saturday and nearly all of Sunday before the big clean-up was finished. She'd washed the widows, washed and ironed and re-hung the curtains, scrubbed and polished the floor, and ended her task with a complete change of bedding, including the difficult washing of the candlewick bedspread which seemed to shed more and more of its tufts as it was rinsed.

Maisie's mother looked on in amazement at her daughter's determination. She didn't know what had gotten into the girl, but she liked the results. She'd been meaning to give Maisie's room a 'going over' for weeks now, but hadn't had the energy.

By the time she was finished, Maisie was whacked.

"Cuppa," her mother suggested.

Maisie nodded, almost too tired to speak.

Maisie sipped the tea gratefully, accompanied by a digestive biscuit. "You've done well, lass," her mother said, filling her own cup and joining Maisie at the biscuit tin, "and as a reward for all your hard work," she continued, proudly, "keep next Friday's board money for yourself."

Maisie couldn't believe her ears. "You mean it?"

Mrs Green nodded. "We'll manage," she said, "just this once mind, but I've talked it over with your dad, we'll manage."

Maisie could have hugged her mother and began to realise that if you worked hard enough and tried hard enough, good things **did** happen, even to her.

She'd meant to see Chrissie today, but the only thing she managed was a bath and bed in her very neat, very clean bedroom. Satisfied with life and herself, Maisie fell asleep.

-----oOo-----

Chapter 10

"What happened to you on Sunday," Chrissie asked, as they made their way into work.

"Nothing much," said Maisie, "just changing my life."

"Changing your what?"

Maisie smiled. "I'll tell you later, but just so you know, from now on, it's all going to be about ME."

Maisie couldn't wait to tell Chrissie her plans and hurried her along the queue for soup and pies, to a table in the corner of the canteen.

She explained about the bedroom plan which, thanks to Chrissie's mum, just might come to pass.

"Then there's this 'mop' she continued, indicating the brittle beehive hairdo. "This," she said in a low voice, "is going to go."

Chrissie raised her eyes to Maisie's crowning glory.

"For a start, she said, "it's getting cut and then........I'm going BLONDE."

Chrissie's eyes widened further, remembering Keiller's dance, when Maisie had tried to look like Diana Dors and how that had ended!

"BLONDE," she echoed, but you're hair's lovely the colour it is."

Chrissie had always envied Maisie's wavy brown hair and couldn't begin to understand why she wanted to change anything about it.

Maisie dismissed the compliment with a wave of her hand.

"That's as maybe, but it says in 'Red Letter' that 'blondes have more fun,' and that's what I intend to have in my life, MORE FUN."

There, she inwardly patted herself on the back, she'd just made another change in her life and her confidence in her 'life-changing' decisions grew.

"Mum's letting me keep my board money this week, so I'll book an appointment with Sylvia's Salon in Albert Street for Saturday and then, look out world, the new Blonde Maisie Green is coming to town."

Chrissie wasn't at all sure about the 'new blonde' Maisie Green, but had to admit, her friend had taken a few hard knocks of late and maybe her new thinking was just what was needed.

Maisie couldn't wait till Saturday and her visit to Sylvia's Salon and, by the end of the week, Chrissie had some more good news for her.

"Mum says she's got the stuff you wanted and that dad will bring it round in his car after teatime tonight."

"Really!" Maisie exclaimed, not able to believe her luck.

Chrissie nodded. "Yep," she said, glad to see her friend's delighted face, "she said the daughter of one of her pals at the WI got married recently and she's clearing out her bedroom, so it looks like your luck's in." Maisie clasped her hands and looked heavenward, "thanks," she said, "to whoever you are up there for liking me."

Chrissie's dad, John Dalton, pulled up at the gate in his Morris Clubman and began unloading Maisie's 'new bedroom'. She ran to open the front door and couldn't believe her eyes.

"Is this all for me?" she asked, searching Mr Dalton's face for reassurance.

"It is that, Maisie," he said kindly, "so if you'll give me a hand, we'll get it moved in."

Chrissie's dad carried the chair and bedside cabinet, while Maisie brought in the rest.

"How much do I owe Mrs Dalton," she asked, searching for her purse in her handbag.

"A couple of quid, I think she said."

Maisie looked around at her new treasures. "For all this?"

"For all this," he echoed, "and see you enjoy it."

After he'd gone, Maisie's mother put her head round the door of her daughter's bedroom, "What was all that about?"

Maisie grinned. "It's about making changes," she said, "today my bedroom, tomorrow, ME."

Maisie's mother inspected the new additions, as Maisie told her about Mrs Dalton and the WI.

"Remind me to go to their next jumble sale," she said, stunned at the 'good as new' pieces, "your dad could do with a new chair."

Maisie spent the rest of the evening, arranging her room.

The opaque glass bowl replaced her old lampshade, the pink padded chair was set in place of the basket chair and the little pink and cream shag pile rug was placed on the floor beside her bed. The bedside cabinet with its soft cream lamp replaced the old wooden chair that had held her alarm clock, but, best of all, a beautiful pink satin quilt and pillowcase now adorned her bed. Maisie had never seen anything so beautiful in her life and stood back, hands on hips, admiring it all.

Slowly, she sat down on the padded chair and took out a cigarette from its packet. She was about to light up, when she realised that smoking in her bedroom was no longer a good idea. She couldn't bear the thought of filling her new space with smoke. Another decision had just been made. Maisie was stopping smoking, as from NOW.

She put the cigarette back into its packet. She'd give them to Chrissie tomorrow and feeling very righteous and pleased with all her decisions, she prepared for bed by the light of the bedside lamp and her toes wiggling in the shag pile rug.

She couldn't wait till tomorrow and the visit to Sylvia's Salon.

Sylvia herself was to do the cutting and colouring, Maisie was told, as she was prepped for her transformation by Gloria, who was responsible for shampooing and tea making.

With her hair swathed in a towel and cup of tea to hand, Maisie waited for the attentions of Sylvia's experienced hands.

"Hepburn or Monroe," she asked Maisie.

Not sure what she meant, Maisie opted for Hepburn.

She watched with a mixture of fascination and apprehension as her locks were snipped and dropped all around her till what remained clung to her scalp in shock.

"It's a bit short," she ventured nervously.

"It's what you asked for," replied Sylvia, "a Hepburn, or as we call it in the trade, an Urchin Cut."

Maisie nodded slowly, beginning to panic that her biggest decision wasn't turning out to be her best one. Ignoring any further queries, Sylvia produced a frightening looking tray of bottles and metal dishes and donned rubber gloves. "This might sting a bit," she said cheerily, "but that's normal." She began to mix the lotions while Maisie closed her eyes. She'd come this far, there was no turning back now. For the next hour, Sylvia applied her hairdressing skills and expertly turned Maisie into a Blonde.

The Green Years

When she finally opened her eyes, Maisie barely recognised herself. Her long dark hair was now very blonde and 'spiky' with varying lengths of fringe falling over her brow.

Maisie stared. "I like it," she said, relief washing over her, "it's just what I wanted," she added, "a new ME."

Sylvia was very pleased with her client's reaction, as she rang up the huge sum of £3. 10/-. Maisie paid up, not only would she be stopping smoking this week, she'd be stopping eating as well to pay for her new look. But it was worth it, she decided, she couldn't wait to show Chrissie.

All the way home, Maisie tried to gauge the reaction of her fellow passengers on the bus to her short blonde hair. She'd deliberately sat downstairs to avoid any smoke, but apart from a sideways glance from the conductor as he took her fare, no one else seemed bothered.

Slightly miffed, she knocked at Chrissie's door, "Taaaraaa," she piped as her friend opened it. For a few seconds, Chrissie really didn't recognise Maisie, but when she did, her reaction was exactly what Maisie had hoped for. They hurried to Chrissie's room. "It's amazing" was all Chrissie kept saying. "Here," she said, offering up a packet of Senior Service, "I think this calls for a ciggie."

Maisie held up her hand. "Thanks, but no thanks," she said, firmly, "I've stopped." She rummaged in her handbag and handed Chrissie her packet of Senior Service. For the second time that morning, Chrissie was amazed.

"But……," she began, but Maisie was having none of it.

"No buts," she said, "no more ciggies for me, I don't want my blonde hair turning yellow with nicotine."

"Sure," Chrissie said, uncertainly, returning the cigarettes to their packet, "I wouldn't want yellow hair either."

"So," Maisie continued, unaware that she was leaving Chrissie behind in her rapid progress to perfection.

"How about we go on the Monkey Parade this Sunday," she asked eagerly, "show them what we've got."

Chrissie felt plain and boring beside Maisie and her new look. "Show them what YOU'VE got you mean," she said quietly, "I've got nothing to show off."

For a minute Maisie didn't understand. Chrissie had plenty to show off about, but then it dawned on her, she'd been so absorbed in her new 'all about me' lifestyle, she'd forgotten that, for Chrissie, things hadn't changed, they were still the same.

"Oh, Chrissie," she whispered, taking her friend's hand in hers, "it's not like that, it's just me trying to be different so that things can change for me, that's all."

Chrissie shrugged. "You've always been the pretty one she said as she hung down her head, "I suppose I'm just a wee bit scared that we'll not be friends when you're mixing with the bonnie crowd."

Maisie whooped, "are you daft or what?" she asked, "what bonnie crowd is this you're talking about, Kenny Wilson, Rab Skelly, Shug Reilly and the like!"

Chrissie couldn't help but giggle, "no," she said, now brightening, "I meant Marty Wilde and Lonnie Donnigan."

Both girls dissolved into a fit of laughter.

"C'mon," Maisie said, "just be happy for me Chrissie, you know we'll always be the best of' pals, FOREVER."

Chrissie grinned, "so, it's the Monkey Parade this Sunday," she said, "you and me, showing them what's what."

"You bet," said Maisie, turning to go, "we'll knock 'em dead."

-----oOo-----

The Green Years

Chapter 11

The Monkey Parade was in full swing when Maisie and Chrissie joined in. Although the wind was keen and Maisie felt the blast of it on her neck, nothing was going to make her cover up her blonde halo.

"Are you not cold," Chrissie asked, wrapping her woollen scarf tighter round her neck. "Freezing" admitted Maisie, "but you have to sometimes suffer for the sake of beauty."

Chrissie nodded in agreement, glad now that she wasn't a 'stunner.'

"Let's hurry up and get to the Palais," Maisie said, "get warmed up." Once inside the dance hall, they felt immediately warmer and Chrissie quickly unfurled her scarf. "That's better," she said, looking round her, "anyone looking?"

Maisie pretended indifference. "Let them look," she said, "as long as they don't try to touch," she added, meaningfully.

But the first one to 'twig' to Maisie's new look wasn't a lad.

"What's all this then, Maisie Green?" Betty Morrison said, loudly, nudging her pals to come and have a look at Maisie's blonde hair.

"Keep moving" Maisie whispered to Chrissie. "Just a bit of a change, that's all," she said over her shoulder, but Betty Morrison persisted. "Who's the lucky lad then?" she said, giving Maisie a hefty nudge in the back, "might it be the lovely Kenny Wilson?"

Maisie felt her face heating up, as annoyance built in her mind. "It's you that fancies Kenny Wilson," she said pointedly, "not me, so if you don't mind……"

The rebuff was like a red rag to a bull and Betty pulled Maisie round to face her.

"I DO mind actually," she shouted, "and if you think Kenny Wilson would have anything to do with a PEROXIDE BLONDE, you've got another think coming."

Before the situation escalated into a full-blown cat fight, two of the patrolling dance hall ushers rushed over and separated the girls.

"Hold up, now hen," one said to Betty, firmly placing himself between the two girls, while the other one held onto Maisie, "remember you're a lady."

"LADY!" Chrissie interjected gamely, her face a picture of incredulity, "she's not a lady!"

By now, the walking crowd had stopped walking and were enjoying the unfolding drama.

"Is that not Maisie Green?" Rab said to Kenny. Kenny strained his neck to see where Rab was pointing. "No way," said Kenny, "Maisie's not a blonde, she's got brownish hair."

Rab squinted into the dimness. "IT IS HER," he insisted, "her hair's different, but it's Maisie Green alright."

The two lads watched as Betty Morrison was ushered downstairs to the cafe to 'cool off,' accompanied by her clutch of 'eggers on.'

"Let's go," Kenny said urgently, "Maisie needs our attention."

Maisie was shaken, but her hair was intact. "C'mon," she said to Chrissie, "let's get out of here before she comes back up."

The Green Years

The girls headed for the door, going against the flow of the walkers, who nodded to them in solidarity, as they hurried on through the gap that was opening up before them.

"I think they feel sorry for us," Chrissie said, as they reached the exit, "that Betty Morrison's a bit of a bruiser."

"Sorry about that girls," said the doorman, pushing open the door for them to pass through, "I hope it doesn't deter you from comin' to the Palais de Dance in future?"

Maisie and Chrissie exchanged incredulous looks. It was doubtful if either of them would return at all and definitely not to the Monkey Parade.

Kenny Wilson and Rab finally caught up with them in the Nethergate.

"Are you two OK?" Kenny asked, taking Maisie's arm. "And you look beautiful, by the way, Maisie."

"Is that your way of asking after our health?" Maisie countered, allowing her eyes to travel slowly from the tip of his toes to the top of his head, before settling on his face.

There it was, the usual expression of fake concern and puppy eyes, but this time, Maisie wasn't taken in. "We saw what happened," Rab interjected, "and we were worried for the both of you." He turned his eyes to Chrissie.

"I'll see you safely home, if you like, Chrissie," Rab added tentatively, with what seemed like genuine concern.

"And leave my friend with HIM?" Chrissie said, pulling at Maisie's sleeve.

All eyes were now fixed on Kenny Wilson.

Once again, Kenny had been wrong-footed by a woman and he didn't like it one bit. How could he be getting things so wrong?

Maisie Green was really bugging him now, from being 'chased' by women, he had become the 'chaser' but Maisie Green wasn't for catching.

The girls moved off, without a backward glance, leaving a deflated Rab and silent Kenny in their wake.

"Do you think Betty Morrison will cause bother tomorrow?" Chrissie asked, once they were settled on the bus.

Maisie shrugged. "Not if she wants to keep her job, she won't."

"What's you next big plan," Chrissie continued, changing the subject.

"Keep fit," Maisie said instantly, anticipating a return-match with Betty Morrison. "All we seem to do is to go dancing and maybe it's time to join a club or something."

"What kind of a club?"

Maisie pondered this. "Sort of sports club, or place where there's an 'activity', other than dancing."

Both girls turned their minds to the problem.

"How about swimming" suggested Chrissie.

Maisie pointing to her blonde locks knocked that idea on the head.

"Athletics?" said Chrissie, "there's a running club at Caird Park."

"In these shoes?" Maisie replied, raising her stilettos with their 3" heels to show Chrissie the impossibility of anything 'athletic'. No glamorous woman would be seen dead in running shoes.

"I'll sleep on it," said Maisie, as they alighted at their stop, "and thank your mum again for helping me with the room, she's one in a million."

Chrissie beamed. She did have a lovely mum and dad and knew how lucky she was.

Her mum was waiting up for her, as usual, when she returned home. She never made any fuss over it, but just couldn't sleep till Chrissie was safely home. Stories of teddy boys and gangs of lads getting into fights were in the

The Green Years

news every day and although, like Maisie, her daughter would soon be seventeen, it still worried her.

"Good fun on your Monkey Walk?" she asked, aware that it was only nine o'clock.

"Not really," said Chrissie, "Maisie's got a new blonde hairdo and I think one of the girls from Keiller's was a bit jealous, so we came home early." She didn't elaborate further.

"Maisie wants to join a sports club now," Chrissie continued, following her mother into the kitchen for a cup of hot chocolate.

"There's no stopping her, is there," said Grace Dalton, mixing the cocoa powder with a little cold milk and putting the rest in a saucepan to heat. "She seems determined to change everything about her life and all at once! What does her mother say about it all?"

Chrissie shrugged, Maisie's mother seemed happy to let her daughter find her own way in life. "By the way, Maisie says thanks again for the stuff, her room's great now."

Grace poured the hot milk into the mugs and stirred gently.

"Here," she handed one of the mugs to her daughter.

"And what about you Chrissie," she said, "what's changing in your life?"

Was now the time to tell her mother about Tommy Murphy?

Chrissie decided against it. "I'm going to join a sports club," she announced, "well, me and Maisie, that is. We've decided to get fit." Mrs Dalton tried not to smile. "Are you sure you need to get fit?" she asked, "you look pretty fit to me."

Chrissie sipped her chocolate drink. "Well, we don't want to get THAT fit, just something that'll be a change from the dancing."

"Well, in that case," her mother said, "why don't the pair of you take up Badminton?"

Chrissie raised her eyebrows.

"Isn't that for lads?" she said.

"Not at all," said her mother, "it's for everyone and there's a Badminton Club at the church hall every Tuesday. They supply the rackets and things and you just turn up."

Now this sounded like something that both of them could do. She'd speak to Maisie about it at work on Monday.

Badminton, she thought, I think I'd like that.

She drained the last dregs of the hot chocolate and headed for bed.

"You know, Maisie thinks you're one in a million," she said sweetly, "and you know what...."

"What?" her mother asked.

"I think she's right."

Grace Dalton beamed. Her daughter was one in a million too, she decided and she was glad she was going to join the Badminton Club, too much dancing at such a young age had always worried her.

-----oOo-----

Chapter 12

The idea of joining a Badminton Club appealed to Maisie greatly. She had seen the girls playing at the tennis club on Forfar Road as she'd passed on the bus. All white skirts and tops with ankle socks and white tennis shoes. She could just picture herself all in white and now, with her short blonde hair keeping her cool, she wouldn't even break sweat!

Reality, however, once again interrupted her reverie. She didn't have any white clothes or tennis shoes for that matter and she certainly didn't have any money to buy anything new.

She broke the news to Chrissie at their tea break in the canteen.

"I'll check with mum tonight," Chrissie said, "but I don't think it matters really. It's not like a REAL Badminton Club, it's only the Fintry church hall."

Just then, Betty Morrison came to their table.

She leaned into Maisie's face. "Hutchie wants to see YOU," she said, her face wearing an unbecoming scowl.

Maisie felt her blood run cold. Mrs Hutchieson was the Supervisor and if she wanted to see Maisie, it could mean only one thing. Betty Morrison had been stirring it, the wee Clipe.

"Do you think Betty Morrison has been saying something about our smoke breaks in the toilets?" Maisie considered this. "Then, she'd want to see both of us, wouldn't she?"

Maisie stood up, leaving all thoughts of Badminton behind her and quickly headed back to her workplace and Mrs Hutchieson's wrath. If she was going to be fired, the quicker she got it over with the better.

"You wanted to see me Mrs Hutchieson?"

"Maisie," smiled the Supervisor, "sit down won't you."

Maisie sat. If this was how you were told you were sacked, it wasn't what she'd imagined it would be like.

"You're seventeen in a couple of weeks I believe?" Mrs Hutchieson asked. Maisie nodded.

"And you do know that Ella Smart's going to be leaving us soon to have her first bairn?"

Maisie nodded again. Ella Smart was the Bonus Checker for the department, but what her pregnancy had to do with Maisie, she just couldn't imagine!

Mrs Hutchieson pulled up her chair alongside Maisie.

"I've been watching you for a while now," she said, "and I like what I see Maisie. You're never late, always clean and tidy and you always get your table cleared of boxes by the end of your shift."

"Thanks," said Maisie, wondering where all this cosy conversation was leading.

As if she'd read Maisie's thoughts, Mrs Hutchieson continued,

"I know well that you're young," she said, "but by the time Ella leaves us at Christmas, you'll be seventeen, which is quite old enough to become our new Bonus Checker."

Maisie's eyes widened in disbelief, "but, what about Betty Morrison, she's a year older........"

Mrs Hutchieson stopped her from going any further.

"I considered Betty for the job, but I think she's more suited to the packing and I've told her so."

The Green Years

"Now," Mrs Hutchieson said decisively, "what do you say, would you like to be our next Bonus Checker?"

Maisie gulped. "If you say I can do it," she said, "then I'd like nothing better."

"Good," said the supervisor, "then that's settled. I'll see Mr Pratt this afternoon and get things moving." She extended her hand and Maisie carefully extended hers in return.

"Welcome to the staff," Mrs Hutchieson said, warmly "and, of course, there'll be a bigger wage packet for you as well."

Maisie almost floated back to her work table as Chrissie and the rest of the packers came back from their tea break.

She tried to indicate to Chrissie that she wasn't going to be sacked, but all would be explained at dinner time.

Maisie couldn't wait to break the news to Chrissie. It seemed the more she helped herself the more help came from all around her. And to be on Keiller's staff at seventeen was a massive achievement in itself. She looked over at Betty Morrison, but all she could see was the top of her cap-covered head. Maisie smiled to herself, she was going places, but Betty Morrison was always going to remain a chocolate packer.

Chrissie was stunned at Maisie's news. "When do you start?" she asked, a bit awestruck by her friend's good fortune.

"Soon," Maisie said, "sometime before Christmas. Ella's going to show me the ropes before she goes."

"Are you no scared Maisie?"

"What's to be scared of?"

"Getting it wrong?"

"The only thing I get wrong, is picking the wrong men!" she exclaimed, "this is work and work I can handle."

Sandra Savage

She sat back and listened to the buzz around her in the canteen. Were they speaking about her, she wondered, and her promotion over Betty Morrison?

She had almost forgotten about the Badminton plan till Chrissie reminded her.

"Are you still wanting to go tomorrow?" she asked Maisie, conscious that her friend seemed to be drifting away from her again into a new world where she didn't fit in.

Maisie refocused her attention. "I do," she said, "it's just that I've nothing sporty to wear."

"Neither have I," said Chrissie, "let's just go and see what's needed once we're there."

Maisie was in such a good mood, she readily agreed. Maybe her mum would have some ideas what to wear, especially when she told her about her promotion and the extra money she'd be bringing in soon.

Chrissie ate her pie and cake, while Maisie sipped her tea.

The hairdo had left her 'skint' till next pay day, but it was all going to be worth it, she was now more sure of that than ever.

As soon as she got home, she headed straight for the bread bin and made herself a jam sandwich. "Hey," called out her mother, "leave room for your tea."

Maisie scoffed the sandwich in seconds. "I've something to tell you," she said, unable to keep the excitement out of her voice.

Mrs Green looked over the rim of her glasses at her daughter. "It'd better be good," she said, "making all this fuss."

"I'm going be the new Bonus Checker at Keiller's," she stated proudly, "what do you think of that?"

Maisie's enthusiasm was catching. "I'm thinking you're a clever wee lassie, Maisie Green, well done," she said a smile adding a few more lines to her face.

"And," Maisie continued, "the best bit is there's more money in it." Maisie's mother almost cried. She'd been desperately thinking of ways to make ends meet for weeks now, as her husband's bad back showed no sign of easing enough for him to return to work and now here was Maisie, coming to the rescue.

"When do you start?" her mother asked.

"In a couple of weeks I think, once I've turned seventeen."

Her mother silently thanked God. Her prayers had been answered. Thanks to her daughter bringing in extra money, Christmas wouldn't be so bad after all.

Maisie delved into the bread bin again. "Can I have another one till the tea's ready?" she asked, laying the slice of bread on the table and waving the knife over the margarine. How could she refuse her anything, "and when you've finished your jammy piece, go through and tell your dad the good news, while I make your tea."

That night, everything in the Greens household beamed, Maisie's mum and dad, Maisie herself and even the furniture seemed to glow with hope for the future. Maisie was on her way and nothing was now going to stop her.

-----oOo-----

Chapter 13

Chrissie met Maisie at the bus stop, a brown paper bag clutched to her chest.

"What's that?"

"I'll show you on the bus," Chrissie whispered, "it's from mum."

Maisie following Chrissie up to the top deck, so she could have her ciggie before going into Keiller's. Maisie had been without cigarettes for two weeks now and, apart from the one slip when she'd pinched one of her dad's, she'd never missed them.

Chrissie lit up her ciggie and handed Maisie the bag. "Look inside," she said, grinning from ear to ear.

Maisie drew out a cream coloured skirt which had been divided into what looked like a pair of very wide shorts. "What's this?"

"They're called Cullottes," Chrissie said knowingly, "mum bought them ages ago to wear at her keep fit class, but she never went."

"And, she's giving them to ME?"

Chrissie nodded. "I've got a pair of Peddle-Pushers to wear, from when I had the bike, so we should be able to play Badminton just fine."

Maisie had almost forgotten about the Badminton, with all her exciting news. She really had lost interest in going, but Chrissie seemed so keen, she felt she couldn't let her down.

The Green Years

She replaced the garment in its bag, it was her suggestion after all and, who knew, she might like it.

"What time does it start?" she asked Chrissie, who seemed to know everything about the whole Badminton thing.

"Half past seven," replied Chrissie, stubbing out the cigarette with her shoe, "so I'll see you at seven?"

Everything seemed to have been arranged and all Maisie had to do was turn up.

"I'll be ready," she said, holding up the paper bag, "hope they fit."

When she got home she showed the Cullotes to her mother.

"I remember them," said Esther Green, the posh girls from the Morgan Academy used to wear them to play Hockey.

"Well," said Maisie, "they'll have to do till payday, but I don't expect we'll be going every week, or anything like that anyway."

Maisie's mother stopped setting the table. "So, why go at all?" she asked.

"It's Chrissie who wants to go," Maisie said, "and I didn't want to let her down by changing my mind at the last minute. She doesn't have a plan like me, you see," she continued, shrugging her shoulders and scanning the kitchen for anything edible.

"Oh yes," Mrs Green said, "and what plan is this?"

Maisie sighed. "Haven't you noticed anything different about me?"

"What, apart from the scarecrow look you're so pleased with?"

Maisie fluffed up her short crop of hair and leaned into the mirror by the window. "It's an URCHIN CUT," she stated firmly "and it's all the rage."

Mrs Green returned to the table setting to conceal a smile. Her daughter was her pride and joy but, sometimes, she didn't understand her one little bit.

"Keep your hair on!" she said, grinning at Maisie's pained expression, "you look beautiful, a real Audrey Hepburn."

Placated, Maisie held up the cullotes. "I'd better go and try these on," she said, warily, "maybe if I put a belt with them, they'll do," she added, making her way to her room.

Esther Green shook her head, Badminton, she pondered, whatever next. She stirred the pot of mince and carrots and tried to remember the last time she'd done anything different. Life was one long domestic chore for Esther Green and, unless a miracle happened, it would be the same for Maisie, whether she played Badminton or not.

Maisie and Chrissie arrived at the Church Hall a bit early to give themselves a chance to have a look round. Two badminton nets had been stretched across the room and they could see some rackets and shuttlecocks on one of chairs that were ranged around the wall.

"Do you think anyone else will turn up?" whispered Maisie, now doubting her decision to come and feeling a bit silly in her cullotes and plimsoles.

"Of course they will," assured Chrissie, sounding a bit uncertain.

"Maybe we should just start?" said Maisie, picking up a racket and shuttlecock.

"You can't just START," ordered Chrissie, nervously, "maybe these rackets belong to someone.

"Can I help you?" A female voice sounded behind them.

Maisie and Chrissie turned round to face a tall, fair haired girl, wearing a black short-sleeved top, black shorts and black plimsoles.

The Green Years

"We want to join," Chrissie said, not sure of herself at all, "is that alright?"

The girl smiled. "Of course," she said, extending her hand. "I'm Fiona," she told them, "Fiona Campbell and you are......?"

Chrissie shook her hand. "I'm Chrissie Dalton," she said "and this is my friend, Maisie Green."

Maisie nodded her greeting without the handshake.

"We want to get fit," she said, "and we thought that Badminton would be a good idea."

Everything in Maisie was saying otherwise. She didn't like the musty atmosphere of the hall, or the echoing that accompanied every noise, but most of all, she didn't like Fiona Campbell. She didn't know why, but could feel a shimmer of jealousy at the confident girl in front of her, with her matching outfit and long slim legs.

Despite her own 'glamorous' image, Maisie felt that the cullotes and brown stripy top she wore made her feel more like something the cat had dragged in and not the athletic sportswoman she had envisioned for herself.

Fiona handed them each a racket and one shuttlecock.

"You can pay at teabreak," she said, when the Treasurer gets here, "and you can use this court," she added pointing to the netted area.

Reluctantly, Maisie took her place on one side of the net, while Chrissie prepared to Serve the shuttlecock from the other.

Fiona Campbell watched from a chair by the door.

After ten minutes of hitting, missing, running, leaping and gasping for breath, both girls knew that badminton wasn't for weaklings, and Maisie was glad when some more members of the Badminton Club began to trickle in.

Fiona Campbell knew them all and Maisie began to feel even more depressed.

"Are you liking this?" she whispered to Chrissie.

Chrissie shrugged, tweaking at her Peddle Pushers which were beginning to stick to her legs.

"Give it time," she said, "we've only just got here."

Fiona and three other girls, all in black, began a 'doubles' match as Maisie and Chrissie watched. "They're good," stated Chrissie, a bit awestruck. "They've had more practice," said Maisie, "we could be as good as them if we really tried." But Maisie wasn't really in the mood for trying, she just wanted to go home and never come back. Badminton wasn't for her.

Chrissie was fast picking up on Maisie's reluctance. "Look," she said, "let's give it one more go, and if you really don't like it, we won't come back."

Maisie agreed, not wanting to hurt Chrissie's feelings, but at the same time, deciding this wasn't part of her plan at all.

The foursome cleared the court and Maisie and Chrissie tried again, this time, with Fiona and her friends now watching their amateur floundering.

Maisie was about to suggest giving up for good, when the hall door opened and two men came in. Fiona rushed over to them, chattering and smiling and pointing at Maisie and Chrissie.

Maisie tried to ignore the obvious fun Fiona was having at their expense, as she skipped towards them.

"The Treasurer and Captain have arrived," she announced, "so, if you'd like to follow me, I'll introduce you and you can pay your joining fee."

Maisie's face was red and flushed with exertion and the cullotes were making her legs feel hot and uncomfortable. She plucked at the strings of her racquet as she followed Fiona to the side of the hall.

"Here they are," Fiona announced, "two new members."

She stepped aside as the Treasurer asked their names and told them the price of the joining fee.

"My name's Maisie Green," Maisie said, "but I'm not sure if I,...I mean WE, are good enough."

From behind the Treasurer, another voice reached Maisie's ears which sounded familiar but she couldn't place it.

"You're good enough alright," it said, "both of you."

Maisie squinted towards the figure, who was bending over tying his plimsole laces.

Ian Brown stood up, a broad smile on his face, "I'm the Club Captain," he said, "welcome aboard."

Maisie's mouth dropped open. "Club Captain?"

Fiona Campbell, who had been watching the encounter, lost the benign smile she had worn since Maisie and Chrissie had arrived.

"Do you know one another, Ian?"

Ian Brown never took his eyes of Maisie, "you could say that," he replied, "what do you say Maisie?"

Chrissie watched as Maisie tried to cool down and regain her composure.

"I'll say we do," she said, aiming her response at Fiona, "we know one another very well."

Maisie had quickly realised, by the pained expression on Fiona's face that Ian Brown meant a bit more to her than just being the Club Captain.

"Are you two joining or what?" interrupted the Treasurer who had been patiently waiting, pen poised, to enrol Maisie and Chrissie.

"We are," said Maisie decisively, "where do we sign."

"When you come next week, I'll show you the ropes," Ian Brown murmured in Maisie's ear, "but tonight I've a mixed doubles match booked with Fiona."

"Next week, it is," she replied sweetly, paying her joining fee of two shillings over to the Treasurer, as Ian Brown joined a miffed Fiona on the court.

"Thought you hated Badminton," Chrissie said pointedly, paying her money and signing the form.

"And you know what thought did," Maisie grinned,

"it thought WRONG."

The two friends hurried back home.

"Before next week," Maisie announced, "I'll be buying all the black badminton gear. Don't want Ian Brown thinking I've no class."

"So that's what all this is about?" Chrissie asked, stopping Maisie in her tracks. "You're jealous of Fiona Campbell!"

Maisie was shocked by Chrissie's observation. "No I'm NOT," she said, "I just don't like her much, that's all."

"But, WHY don't you like her?"

Maisie shrugged. "Don't know," she said defensively, but Chrissie had hit a nerve. That was what Fiona Campbell had and Maisie didn't. CLASS.

Back to the drawing board, thought Maisie as she pulled on her pyjamas and slipped under the pink satin quilt. She may have a new bedroom, new blonde hair and even, very soon, a new job, but what she didn't have money couldn't buy and that was CLASS.

She switched off her cream coloured lamp. She'd have to sleep on things, there had to be a way to become more like Fiona Campbell. That night, Maisie dreamed all of her teeth fell out and was relieved to waken up and find them intact.

Today, she would re-think her plan.

-----oOo-----

Chapter 14

"Maisie, Maisie," called Chrissie before she'd even reached the bus stop. She was waving something in her hand.

"LOOK!" she exclaimed, excitedly, "it's a letter from Tommy."

Chrissie's happiness was infectious and the whole of the bus queue began smiling.

"Calm down," said Maisie smiling, "what's got your knickers in a twist, this early in the morning?"

The arrival of the bus halted any further talk till they were sitting in their seats and Chrissie was unfolding the sheet of cream paper from its cream envelope.

"Tommy's ship is coming in to Dundee for maintenance and it's this weekend." She clasped the letter to her heart. "Isn't it WONDERFUL!"

Maisie grinned. "Only the most wonderful thing I've ever heard," she teased.

Chrissie turned huge bright eyes onto Maisie.

"You know what this means, don't you?" she breathed.

Maisie feigned ignorance. "Nooooo."

Chrissie nudged her hard on the arm. "It means," she said in hushed tones, "I'll know this weekend if Tommy loves me, I mean really loves me, like he's been saying in his letters."

Maisie felt a mix of hope and compassion for her friend. Based on her own experiences with men, she couldn't quite believe that Tommy Murphy would prove the exception to the rule.

She linked her arm into Chrissie's, "I'm sure Tommy loves you," she lied "and remember who you're going to pick as your bridesmaid then the two of you get married," she added, trying to keep her words light. But inside, Maisie wasn't at all sure of Tommy Murphy's intentions at all.

She had thought Jack Carter was a man to trust and how wrong she had been about that and how much it had hurt. Please don't let Chrissie be let down as well, she silently prayed to whoever maybe listening.

Without wanting to, her thoughts turned to Ian Brown. She thought he was nice, but again, how could she tell. Then there was Fiona Campbell, how could she compete against her for Ian Brown's attentions and did she even want to? The two girls spent the rest of the journey to work lost in their own thoughts, and Maisie realising that she hadn't even begun to formulate a Plan B to become CLASSY.

"C'mon," Chrissie said, "our stop."

Maisie brought her mind back to work. Mrs Hutchieson was to have spoken to their Manager, Willie Pratt about her becoming a Bonus Checker and today she'd find out if he'd OK'd it. But Maisie needn't have worried, Mrs Hutchieson called her over the minute she came to her table.

"It's all arranged," she told Maisie, "next week, you're to work with Ella, she'll show you what to do and then two weeks from now, you'll take over the job by yourself."

Mrs Hutchieson beamed at Maisie. "I've put my reputation on the line to get you this job," she said, "so don't let me down."

The Green Years

Maisie stood up, proudly, "thank you Mrs Hutchieson," she said, "for everything you've done for me and I won't let you down."

Head held higher than normal, Maisie returned to her work table. She had carefully worded her thanks with what she called a 'posh' voice, just like the one she'd heard Fiona Campbell use. That was what made people classy, she realised, it was the way they spoke!

Plan B began to form. Maisie decided she would practice speaking like Fiona till she sounded just like her. Simple.

For the rest of the week, Maisie and Chrissie lived in their heads, Chrissie imagining kissing Tommy as he told her he loved her and Maisie practicing her vowels and words ending with 'ing'. This wasn't as easy as she'd hoped, her voice sounding alien to her and she was attracting strange looks from her fellow packers every time she spoke.

"She's turned into a right wee snob since they've made her a Bonus Checker," Betty Morrison was telling anyone who would listen to her. But Maisie persevered, if she was going to reinvent herself, she had to be strong and kept telling herself that if Fiona Campbell could do it, so could she.

Chrissie breezed over to their table in the canteen on the Friday at teabreak. "I can't wait till tomorrow," she said wistfully, "I'm meeting Tommy at the Dock Gates at eleven o'clock and we're going to spend all day TOGETHER."

"All day," Maisie asked, "is your mum alright with that?"

"Oh, she doesn't know," Chrissie whispered, "she thinks the letters I've been getting are from a pen pal in Orkney."

Maisie blinked in surprise. "And she believes that!"

Chrissie hung her head. "I know it's wrong," she said softly, "but I can't tell her about Tommy, not yet anyway, not till I know how he feels."

Maisie suddenly realised just how much Chrissie was banking on Tommy Murphy being 'the one.'

"But what if it doesn't work out as you hope?" she asked covering her friend's hand with her own.

Chrissie pulled her hand away, her eyes bleak and challenging.

"Just because things didn't work out for you Maisie Green, doesn't mean they won't for me."

Maisie was stunned. She'd never seen this side of Chrissie before and wasn't sure how to respond.

"I didn't mean anything, Chrissie," she tried to reassure her, just be careful, that's all....."

Chrissie pushed her chair away from the table and stood up. "I can look after myself," she said defiantly, "and Tommy does love me," she added, "just wait and see."

With these words, Chrissie left a confused Maisie alone in the canteen.

Chrissie hurried back to her work table before any tears could begin. Maisie had touched on her one big fear, that Tommy Murphy had been stringing her along and, when the time came to meet again, he'd see her for what she was, a mousey, boring chocolate packer, with nothing to offer a man of the world like Tommy.

Not wanting to repeat the unsettling experience at the canteen, Chrissie avoided any contact with Maisie for the rest of the day and took a later bus home. Tomorrow would be wonderful she told herself and Maisie Green, well, what did she know about love anyway.

Saturday morning dawned bright and clear as Chrissie prepared for her date with Tommy.

"You look nice," Grace Dalton said, as she scrambled eggs for their breakfast. "Are you meeting Maisie later?"

The Green Years

This was it, the truth or a lie.

"Yes," she lied, "we're going out for the day on the bus to Forfar."

Mrs Dalton's eyes opened a little wider in surprise.

"FORFAR," she echoed, "what's going on there?"

Chrissie began to feel hot and uncomfortable, lying didn't come easily to her and especially lying to her mother.

"Nothing really," Chrissie replied, "we just fancied a change from the Dundee shops, that's all."

Grace Dalton laughed. "Well, in that case, you can bring me back a Forfar Bridie, I'm told they're great."

Chrissie froze. How had she managed to get herself boxed into this corner and now her mother would be expecting her to bring home a Forfar Bridie of all things.

"I'll try," she said, focusing her attention on her eggs and toast and willing her mother to drop the subject of Forfar. She wished she hadn't fallen out with Maisie, she'd have been the perfect cover for her clandestine meeting with Tommy and she just prayed that her mother wouldn't run into her and discover the truth.

By the time the clock was at half past ten, Chrissie was a bag of nerves. She felt nauseous and shaky, if this was what love felt like, she wasn't at all sure if it was for her. Pushing her misgivings out of her mind she closed the front door behind her and caught the bus into Dundee. The walk to the Dock Gates at Dock Street, helped to settle her stomach a bit, but her legs were still wobbling when she crossed the wide road leading to her fate.

Chrissie's fears vanished as Tommy Murphy waved and ran towards her. He gathered her up in his arms and held her tightly. "I was scared you wouldn't come," he said huskily, "I've been waiting here since ten o'clock."

"I was scared you wouldn't come," Chrissie told him, giggling at her nerves and the now ridiculous notion that Tommy didn't care about her.

Keeping his arm around her waist, Tommy guided her out of the gates. "Where do you want to go?" he asked, grinning.

"Forfar," came the immediate reply.

"Where's that?" asked a perplexed Tommy, barely knowing Dundee, never mind this place called Forfar.

"It's in the country," Chrissie said, "we can get a bus from the bus station and have Forfar Bridies for our dinner."

Tommy had never heard of Forfar Bridies either, but if that's what Chrissie wanted to do, then that's what they'd do.

"Lead the way," he said, "I don't care where we go, as long as we're together." Chrissie's whole body thrilled to the words.

Tommy Murphy really, really, loved her. She was as sure as a girl could be about that.

Maisie spent her Saturday shopping for her Badminton outfit. The next time she went to the club, she would be properly dressed and, besides, Ian Brown had said they'd be playing together and she was determined not to 'show herself up' by wearing Chrissie's mother's cullotes and her old school sandshoes. And then, there was Fiona Campbell, with her posh voice and all black out-fit. No, she would need to 'up her game' for next Tuesday.

She was sifting through a range of sporty looking tops in DM Browns department store, when Mrs Dalton tapped her on the shoulder.

"Why, Maisie," she said, "I didn't expect to see you here, I thought you and Chrissie were going to Forfar for the day."

Maisie was lost for words. FORFAR, what had Chrissie told her mother?

"Well," Maisie began, trying to find the right words to say to cover for Chrissie, who she knew was with Tommy Murphy...somewhere! "I wasn't feeling too well...." she began, "so Chrissie went on her own."

Mrs Dalton looked doubtful. "What time was this?" she asked.

Maisie felt more flustered. "Earlier," she said, "when she called round at nine."

Grace Dalton now knew someone was lying, Chrissie had been eating her breakfast at home at nine o'clock.

"So, you weren't feeling well and so Chrissie went, on her own.....to Forfar?"

Maisie nodded. Without another word Grace Dalton turned on her heel and left the shop. She hurried home, her husband would know what to do.

"John," she called, as soon as she'd opened the door to their home, "something terrible had happened to Chrissie."

-----oOo-----

Chapter 15

John Dalton put down his newspaper and his pipe.

"What are you talking about Grace?"

Mrs Dalton flopped down in a chair and began to explain.

"So you see, she's not with Maisie at all, she's gone to Forfar on her own..... or with someone else, a STRANGER!"

Even as she said it, Grace Dalton felt a wave of panic building in her heart.

Not normally given to high emotion, John Dalton could see how worried his wife was and his practical side took over.

"I'll get the car," he said, "Forfar's not a big place, we'll find her."

They hurried out to the car and set off on the road to Forfar in search of their young daughter, with John Dalton sure they would find Chrissie and Grace Dalton fearing the worst.

But Chrissie was oblivious to the furore that was about to find her and was happily wandering through the streets of the small market town with her man.

They'd stopped at a little gift shop and Tommy had bought her a silver bracelet. "So you know you're mine," he'd said, "every time you look at it." Chrissie had never been so happy.

"Now," Tommy announced, as they left the gift shop, "how about those Bridies you talked about, we could get them and find a nice spot for a kind of a picnic." Chrissie nodded.

"There's a little park not far from here," she said, "we could have our picnic there."

Bridies purchased, plus one to take home to her mum, the two lovebirds found a bench in the tiny railed garden and sat closely together while Tommy placed the bracelet on Chrissie's wrist.

"It's the most beautiful thing I've ever seen," she whispered, "and I'll never take it off Tommy, never."

Tommy put his arm around her and pulled her into him.

"Can I kiss you?" he asked.

"You can."

The kiss was so gentle and loving that Chrissie almost cried.

"Are you OK?" Tommy asked, anxiously, seeing her misty eyes.

"I'm just so happy," Chrissie whispered, "being here, with you."

Tommy held her tighter, "then I'll kiss you forever," he said, "I think I love you."

Chrissie thought she would burst with happiness. "And I love you too Tommy Murphy," she murmured into his neck, "forever."

"There she is!" Grace Dalton squealed. Her husband slammed on the brakes. They'd been searching Forfar from the centre out and now, they'd found their daughter and she was being held, against her will, by a STRANGE MAN. Grace's worst fears had been realised and she prayed they weren't too late.

Chrissie was too stunned to register immediately what was happening. Her mother and father came running towards her and Tommy, her mother waving frantically and her dad bringing up the angry rear.

The pair jumped apart and stood up.

"MUM," Chrissie called out, "and DAD," she added her voice trembling with emotion. "What are you doing here?"

John Dalton took his daughter's arm and pulled her away from Tommy's side. "More to the point," he said angrily, "what are YOU doing here, and WHO'S THIS?"

Chrissie burst into tears, while Tommy stood in silence, fully expecting the angry John Dalton to turn on him at any minute.

"It's not what you think mum," Chrissie said her voice pleading to be understood. "He's my boyfriend and we were going to have a picnic here." She held up the bag of Bridies as evidence.

It was Grace Dalton's turn to be stunned. She turned her attention to Tommy Murphy. "BOYFRIEND!" she said in disbelief. Tommy nodded. "I'm on 48 hours leave from my ship the SS Stalwart," he explained, "and I've been writing to Chrissie for weeks now and......" He glanced at Chrissie for confirmation.

"It's true," said Chrissie weakly, "the letters weren't from a pen pal," she confessed, "they were from Tommy."

Grace Dalton didn't know whether to laugh or cry. Her daughter wasn't a little girl anymore, she realised, she was becoming a woman, with all the pleasures and pitfalls that brought.

"C'mon," John Dalton cut in decisively, "let's get you home." He put his arm around Chrissie's shoulder, expecting her to comply as usual, but Chrissie stood her ground.

"Only if Tommy can come too," she said boldly, reaching out for Tommy's hand and finding it.

"What do you say, Grace?" he asked his wife.

Grace could see the new determination in her daughter's eyes and whether she liked it or not, she knew

The Green Years

that 'puppy love' had arrived in her daughter's life and there was nothing she could do about it, but accept.

Grace nodded her agreement and the four of them headed to Fintry, with three Forfar Bridies still intact.

The journey back was mainly silent with Tommy feeling the most uncomfortable. He did think he loved Chrissie, but he hadn't bargained on meeting her parents so soon into the fledgling relationship and couldn't face the thought of the cross-examination he was sure to get when they got back to Chrissie's house.

As soon as he got to familiar territory, he asked to be dropped off at the nearest bus stop.

Chrissie, who had been beginning to relax, felt her muscles tense again. "Don't you want your Bridie?" she asked naively, "mum'll heat them up again in the oven when we get home."

Tommy felt himself sweat. He was being invited to eat with the family!

He searched for polite words to excuse his lack of appetite, but found none, as his eyes were desperately seeking out a bus stop.

"Over there," he said, already opening the door as the car slowed into the kerb. Without another word, his hands sweating and his breathing coming in short gasps, he ran to the other side of the road, disappearing into the waiting queue.

"Well!" Grace exclaimed to her husband, "so much for manners."

The Daltons drove home, each unable to break into the ice that surrounded them with Tommy's rapid departure. John Dalton was just glad that his daughter was safe, Grace Dalton was unhappy that Chrissie had lied to her, while Chrissie sat twirling her silver bracelet round and round her wrist in tearful silence.

The bridies were never eaten as no one had an appetite anymore. The warm and friendly atmosphere that usually prevailed in the Dalton home had somehow dispersed and had been replaced by an uncertainty about the future, especially Chrissie's.

"Will you be seeing him again?" Grace asked gently, aware at how much her daughter was hurting.

Chrissie shrugged her shoulders, her eyes still fixed on Tommy's bracelet.

"Maybe, he'll write soon......" Grace began but Chrissie cut her dead, her eyes like black coals.

"What do you care, if he writes or not," she shouted, tears beginning to flow again, "HE LOVED ME," she said, and I LOVED HIM, and now IT'S ALL OVER."

Chrissie ran from the room. It was all too much and blinded by tears she found herself on Maisie's doorstep.

Maisie didn't have to ask what was wrong, as she guided Chrissie through to her bedroom, it was plain to see that for whatever reason, Tommy Murphy was no more. She sat on the edge of her bed while Chrissie sniffed and gulped and mopped her red-rimmed eyes with her sodden handkerchief.

"Tea?" asked Maisie tentatively.

Chrissie shook her head and rummaged instead into her handbag for her cigarettes.

"Do you mind?" she asked tearfully, indicating the packet.

Maisie did mind, she was now a non-smoker and would have to get rid of the smell of smoke from her bedroom somehow, after Chrissie had gone. But Chrissie's distress won the day.

She smiled and nodded, before crossing the room and opening the window.

"I met your mum in D M Browns today," Maisie began, knowing that somehow that fateful meeting had triggered the unhappiness in front of her, "she said you were at Forfar.........with me?"

Chrissie scrunched her handkerchief into a damp ball. "I know," she said, her eyes never meeting Maisie's. "And I was at Forfar, but I went with Tommy......sorry I lied."

Maisie sighed. "So, what happened?"

"When mum realised I wasn't with you, she panicked and her and dad came looking for me."

"They came to Forfar?"

Chrissie grimaced at the memory. "They found me and Tommy kissing," she looked up at Maisie, her eyes begging understanding, "he loves me Maisie and I love him...and he gave me this." She extended her left arm and pulled up her cardigan sleeve.

Maisie looked closer. "It's a silver bracelet," she whispered, awed at the pretty gift on Chrissie's wrist, "he must really love you to buy you jewellery."

She looked into the eyes of her friend, "so, why so sad?" Maisie asked. "You should be happy to have found a real man who really loves you." Chrissie's head dropped again, just as ash from her cigarette fell onto Maisie's floor.

There was silence as the two girls gazed at the fallen ash.

"Here," Maisie said, handing Chrissie a little trinket dish.

"If he loves me Maisie," Chrissie asked, quietly, "why did he run away?"

The final part of the puzzle fell into place, as Chrissie told of the car ride back from Forfar.

Tommy Murphy may have wanted Chrissie, Maisie surmised, but he didn't want her enough to meet her mum and dad.

"What'll you do now?" she asked, knowing there was no real answer.

Chrissie shrugged and lit another cigarette, inhaling the smoke deeply and blowing it out towards the window in respect for Maisie's pride in her revamped bedroom.

"His ship sails tomorrow," she said, "so unless he comes to find me, he'll be gone by Monday and I'll never see him"............the tears began to flow again.

Maisie looked at her friend, so here it was again, but this time it had happened to Chrissie. Was there no one a girl could trust? Not Kenny Wilson, not Jack Carter, not Tommy Murphy, NO ONE?

"C'mon," she said to Chrissie, "let's get some fresh air and make a plan for the future for YOU." She wasn't at all sure what that plan might be, but her eyes were beginning to smart with the tobacco smoke and her lovely room was almost disappearing into the haze.

Chrissie stood up and threw her arms around Maisie.

"You're the best friend anyone could ever have," she said, hoarsely, "and I'm sorry I shouted at you in the canteen and I'm sorry I lied about Forfar and........are we still friends?"

Maisie unhooked herself from Chrissie's grasp.

"Always," she said, and meant it, "now let's get out of here, tomorrow's another day and, who knows what that will bring."

Chrissie nodded, "Isn't it horrible being sixteen," she said philosophically, "I wish I was nineteen and settled down, then I wouldn't have to go through all this boyfriend stuff and get hurt so much."

"Maybe seventeen will be better" Maisie mused, also not wanting to be hurt again by a man, "but whatever happens," she added, linking her arm into Chrissie's as they stepped out into the sunshine, "we've got each other."

-----oOo-----

The Green Years

Chapter 16

Maisie began her new role as a Trainee Bonus Checker under the watchful eye of the pregnant Ella Smart. "There's a lot to learn" said Ella, "and you've got to be good with your sums."

She looked at Maisie for a nod of agreement before continuing.

Maisie had two weeks to learn the job and then she'd be on her own, so all thoughts about men would be put aside till she conquered the paperwork. She couldn't afford to get any of the packers bonus money wrong, especially not Betty Morrison. She shivered at the thought.

"Right Ella," Maisie said hastily, to the waiting Ella, "I'm good at sums," she said, "and I'm a quick learner."

Ella Smart raised an eyebrow. "You'll need to be," she said, "or the job'll go to Betty Morrison."

Maisie wasn't about to let that happen and focussed her whole attention on the business at hand.

She hadn't had a chance to speak to Chrissie, who'd missed their usual bus and arrived late, but a quick glance was enough to let her know that all was still not well with her friend.

They met up at dinner-time in the canteen.

"Are you in the mood of company," Maisie asked a pensive Chrissie. Her friend shrugged and Maisie sat down opposite her, checking her mince roll for quantity of mince as she did so.

"A bit stingy with the mince," she said, by way of conversation.

There was no response.

"I see you're still wearing the silver bracelet," Maisie said gently, "has Tommy been in touch?"

Chrissie's lips tightened and her eyes began to blur.

No," she whispered, "his ship sailed yesterday." Chrissie took a deep breath, "so that's that, I suppose...." her chin beginning to quiver.

"Oh! Maisie," she whimpered, "how could something so right, go so wrong?"

The figure of Kenny Wilson strolled towards their table.

"Is this a private conversation," he began, directing his question at Maisie, "or can anyone join in, ie ME?"

Maisie's eyes blazed with anger.

"Can't you see we're busy," she hissed, nodding her head towards the silent Chrissie.

Even Kenny Wilson knew when to back off. "Sorry," he said, "just thought I'd say hello.......it's been a while......"

Maisie stared silently at Kenny till he straightened up and made to go. AGAIN, Maisie Green had made him look small.

"Right," he said, turning her attention to Chrissie, "see you around then girls."

Maisie breathed a sigh of relief as Kenny made his departure.

"Ignore him," she said to Chrissie, "he's a loser, along with his mate."

"Help me Maisie," Chrissie suddenly murmured, "I don't know what to do."

The Green Years

Maisie grasped her hand. "Not here," she said, "after work at Wallace's Tearooms Chrissie, we'll put the world to rights again then, OK?"

Chrissie nodded listlessly, and lapsed in silence while Maisie finished her mince roll, her thoughts ranging in circles trying to think of what she was going to say to Chrissie later on to put her heart back together again, for it truly seemed broken.

For the rest of the afternoon, Maisie kept glancing over at Chrissie, but nothing changed. She packed the chocolates on automatic pilot and kept her head down and her eyes fixed on the sweets as she boxed them.

By the time they'd found a table at the tearoom and ordered their usual pie and beans and pot of tea, Maisie had gone beyond pity for her friend and was now feeling angry at how easily Tommy Murphy had turned Chrissie's world upside down with just a few sweet nothings and a bracelet. She had to bring her back to her senses.

They ate in silence, Chrissie's pie tasting of cardboard while Maisie's tasted delicious. She poured the tea.

"What's to do, Chrissie?" she asked kindly. "You remind me of me, after Kenny Wilson laughed at me at Keiller's dance, when my 'Diana Dors bust' landed on the floor." Maisie smiled, hoping it would be infectious, "and look at me now," she said, pointing to her bosoms, "flat as a pancake but still alive and kicking."

There was a glimmer of a smile on Chrissie's lips.

"You're daft as a brush, you are," she said, remembering how they stuck together through Maisie's embarrassment.

"And you ate half my pudding supper too," Maisie added, sensing a breakthrough and allowing her smile to broaden into a grin.

"I know, I know," said Chrissie, becoming a bit more animated, "but Tommy was……..well, I thought Tommy was……the one."

"Well," said Maisie, "it might be that we've a few frogs to kiss yet, before THE ONE eventually turns up."

Chrissie took a sip of her tea. "But," she began, her voice beginning to quiver again, "what if he WAS the one and I've missed the boat, so to speak, realising Tommy had sailed the previous day, so she literally had 'missed the boat.'

"C'mon," said Maisie, sounding more reassuring than she felt, "men are like busses," she said, "you wait for ages for one to come along, then three come along together!"

"Not funny," said Chrissie, but she was smiling again.

"Look," said Maisie, "I know you're hurting and I know you fell for him, but feeling miserable isn't going to bring him back now, is it."

Chrissie shrugged. "I suppose not."

"It's my birthday next week," Maisie said, "how about we celebrate with a night out at………. the THEATRE!" Maisie exclaimed, only thinking of the idea a split second before she said it.

"We'll get dressed up all posh," she said, warming to her theme, "and forget all about men and their promises, what do you say?"

Chrissie was visibly brightening up now. She'd only been to the theatre once and that was with her mum and dad to see a pantomime. But this was different. This would be a real play.

"What's on?" she asked, a tinge of excitement coming into her voice and Tommy Murphy forgotten for the moment.

"It doesn't matter," said Maisie, throwing caution to the wind, "whatever it is, we'll enjoy it, just you and me and no one else."

The Green Years

Maisie lifted her teacup. "Cheers Chrissie," she said, "here's to our night out and better days to come."

A real smile crossed Chrissie's face this time. Maisie was a wonderful friend and she felt so lucky to have her. "Cheers."

By the time the girls had finished their tea, a sort of balance had been restored. Maisie knew it would be some time before Chrissie recovered as, she too, was still smarting from her unhappy experiences with Jack Carter and Kenny Wilson.

"Do you want to go to the Badminton tomorrow," Chrissie asked, as they boarded their bus home.

Maisie thought about it. She had vowed to give men a miss while she was learning the new job and decided to stick to her guns. Besides, Chrissie's heart wouldn't really have been in it and anyway, Maisie wasn't quite ready to meet the posh Fiona Campbell again so soon. "Let's give it a miss this week," she said, "maybe next week, when you're feeling better."

Chrissie nodded, glad they weren't going. Love still hurt.

"I'll get mum to pick up two tickets at the Rep for next Saturday," Maisie called over her shoulder, "and it's on me."

Maisie's mother was watching the TV as usual and balancing a cup of tea in one hand and a doughnut in the other.

"You're late home from work," she said, her eyes flicking momentarily towards her daughter before returning to the screen.

"Chrissie and me had pie and beans at Wallaces," she said, "Chrissie's a bit fed up."

"Oh!"

"Yeah," Maisie said, "so we've decided to go for a night out for my birthday next week and I thought you could maybe do me a favour."

Maisie now had her mother's undivided attention.

"If you want to miss your board money again, the answer's NO," she said emphatically.

"It's nothing like that, "Maisie chided, "I need to get two tickets to the Rep for next Saturday and wondered if you could pick them up for us at the box office?"

"REP," Esther Green echoed, "you're going up in the world, aren't you?"

"Not really," Maisie answered, but secretly she knew different. She was going places and maybe a visit to the theatre would help improve her whole image. After all, she was now a Bonus Checker and a member of a badminton club and she had a lovely new room and as for her hair, well, blondes were entitled to have more fun, weren't they?"

She rummaged in her handbag for her purse and took out two pound notes. She handed them to her mother. "There," she said, "that should be enough, but if it's not, I'll give you the rest when you get the tickets."

"What's on," her mother asked.

"Don't know," said Maisie, "and it doesn't matter anyway, just get the two tickets for next Saturday.......please?"

Mrs Green stuck the money under the ashtray on the little table by her side. "Consider it done," she said and returned to her viewing.

"What's that girl up to now," her husband Joe asked, eventually dragging his eyes away from the news bulletin, "turning into a right little madam in her old age, she is."

Esther Green pursed her lips. "She's just growing up Joe," she said, remembering her own 'green years' when finding the right man had been the only consideration and look where that had led.

She finished her doughnut and lit another cigarette. Maybe Maisie would have more of a life that she'd had and if going to the theatre was what she fancied, who had she, or anyone else for that matter, got the right to criticize her.

Ian Brown had been looking forward since the previous Tuesday to the Badminton Club and his next encounter with Maisie. He'd arrived early, hair cut at the weekend and doused in Old Spice aftershave.

He had to make his move soon, he thought, and tonight he'd make sure Maisie knew he had designs on her.

"Hey," called a female voice, "you're early."

Ian turned to face the advancing form of Fiona Campbell. He had once fancied Fiona, but that was before he'd met Maisie Green. Now, all that had changed for him, but not for Fiona.

"You look smart," Fiona twittered, trying to conceal a flush of admiration for Ian, "going somewhere after the game?"

Ian unzipped his racquet from its case and glanced at his watch. It was gone seven thirty, and the realisation grew that Maisie wasn't coming.

"No," he said, bringing his attention back to Fiona, "just back to work as usual."

"Oh, yes," Fiona remembered, "security at the NCR isn't it?"

Ian sat on one of the chairs around the hall, his eyes flitting to the door every time it opened. But Maisie didn't appear and he got more and more dejected. "Yeah," he said, blandly, "security."

Fiona sat herself down next to him, unsure of herself and Ian's mood. She'd had her eye on him for weeks now, and just when she thought she was getting somewhere, that little minx Maisie Green had shown up and, to Fiona's 'green' eyes, had flaunted herself shamelessly to get his attention. "You look as though you've lost a pound and found a shilling," she said, "is something wrong?"

Ian bounced his racquet against his free hand. Fiona was a lovely looking girl and most men would have jumped at the chance to take her out and although he was aware of her intentions towards him, he no longer responded to them.

Ever since first meeting her, he only had eyes for Maisie and now, he had to accept, she didn't have eyes for him.

He turned to face Fiona's concerned face. "No, Fiona," he said, "nothing's wrong." He extended his hand to help her up from her seat. "C'mon," he said, "let's play."

The exertion helped to work of the adrenalin that had surged through his system with Maisie's non-appearance and by the end of the game he was whacked and grateful for Fiona's offering of a large glass of orange squash.

"What are you doing Saturday?" Fiona asked casually, sipping her own drink and avoiding eye contact with Ian.

"Nothing much."

"Well," Fiona continued boldly, in for a penny in for a pound, "I've got a couple of theatre tickets for the Rep and thought you might like to go.........if you fancy it. Cheer you up a bit."

There was a lengthy pause while Ian thought things through.

He wouldn't be seeing Maisie, that was for sure and Fiona was right, he did need a bit of cheering up."

"That's very friendly of you," he said, pointedly, "I'll pay for the tickets though," he added.

Fiona almost jumped for joy. "No, no, they're already paid for," she said, "dad got them from a colleague of his who had to call off." She was aware she was babbling and was a bit deflated when he had referred to her invite as friendly, but at least, they would be going out TOGETHER, instead of just being part of the group.....and best of all, there would be no Maisie Green.

"Meet outside the Rep then," Ian said, packing up his badminton gear, around seven?"

Fiona nodded, trying to keep the excitement out of her eyes.

"Seven it is."

-----oOo-----

Chapter 17

The working week wore on and although Chrissie had perked up a bit, she still wasn't back to her usual self by the time Friday came round.

"Mum's got the tickets for tomorrow," Maisie said as they walked to the bus stop, "it's a real play too," she continued, trying to build suspense into her words, "by Agatha Christie."

Chrissie stopped walking, "Agatha WHO?"

"Christie," Maisie repeated, not knowing who she was either.

"Who's she?"

Maisie urged Chrissie forward. "Here's the bus," she said, quickly changing the subject, "hurry up or we'll miss it."

"So, I'll come over to your house at half past six," Maisie gushed, "so be ready and dress to impress," she said, as they parted company at their bus stop in Fintry.

Chrissie still wasn't sure about Agatha 'whats'ername', or even what the play was about, but it would maybe take her mind off Tommy for a while. She hoped, anyway, so what had she to lose and it was Maisie's birthday after all.

Maisie looked at the theatre tickets for the first time properly. Stalls, it said, seats G14 and G15. 'Witness for the Prosecution.' Maisie grimaced. This play didn't sound much fun, in fact, she was tempted to cancel the whole thing and go dancing instead, before she realised that now

The Green Years

she'd spent the money on the tickets, there wasn't any left for dancing.

Make the most of it, she told her reflection in the mirror, after all this is another step in my self-improvement programme and, who knows, I might just enjoy it!

She pushed all negative thoughts to the back of her mind and took out the dress she'd worn to Keiller's dance. One of her mum's pals had taken the dress in on her sewing machine, with the addition of several 'darts' and the dress now fitted her natural curves.

There, she thought, as she flicked her blonde hair into little curls around her forehead and donned her cream duster coat, you'll pass.

Chrissie was ready to go when she knocked at her door. She still wasn't speaking much to her mum, but at least she'd stopped blubbing and was looking more like herself.

They hopped on the bus and Maisie showed Chrissie the tickets. 17/6d Chrissie blurted, EACH. She turned amazed eyes on her friend. "Witness for the Prosecution?" she queried, "what does that mean."

Maisie returned the tickets to her handbag. "I think it means.....well.... it's probably about......oh, for goodness sake Chrissie, let's just wait and see."

The rest of the journey was taken in silence, 'til the girls were making their way along Ward Road to the theatre.

"Now remember," Maisie said, her legs tensing as they got nearer the doorway and her grip on Chrissie's arm tightening, "we're sophisticated ladies and theatre goers, so just smile and walk in with the rest of the crowd and don't ask anyone who Agatha Christie is, please?"

The lights from the doorway gleamed out into the evening air as the girls made their approach.

Suddenly, Chrissie pointed to a figure standing near the entrance. "It's Fiona Campbell," she said, loudly, "what's she doing here?" And before Maisie could stop her, she waved to Fiona and made her way towards her, disconnecting herself from Maisie's gripping hand.

"Why Chrissie," cooed Fiona, "and Maisie," she added as Maisie drew alongside her, "how lovely to see you both." She turned to Maisie, "we missed you at the Badminton on Tuesday," she said smoothly, "is everything alright?"

"Fine," said Maisie tightly, "just forgot." She could have kicked herself for the lame excuse. Her newfound sophistication ebbed away as she took in Fiona's dress and fur stole.

"It's my birthday," she hurried on, wishing to end the conversation, "so we'd better get to our seats." She grasped Chrissie's elbow again, as she fell deeper into embarrassment, terrified now that Fiona Campbell would ask her about Agatha Christie.

"I'll maybe see you at the interval then," Fiona added, "Ian and myself will probably be in the bar for a drink as usual."

"IAN," Maisie gasped, "Ian Brown, is he here?"

Fiona smiled. "Well, you didn't think I'd be here on my own, did you?"

Chrissie suddenly made the connection and quickly ushered the silent Maisie away from her nemesis and into the theatre.

How they got to their seats Maisie didn't know, she only knew that Fiona Campbell had won. Ian Brown was her boyfriend.

A nudge from Chrissie alerted her to the arrival of Ian Brown and Fiona.

Maisie watched as the pair walked past them down the aisle to the second row from the front, but within minutes

The Green Years

of their arrival the theatre lights dimmed, blocking them from view and the play began.

Maisie tried to concentrate on the action on stage, but her mind wouldn't let her. All she could think of was Ian Brown and how he'd proven to her, yet again, that men couldn't be trusted and when the interval came, all she wanted was to go home.

"Not much of a play," she suggested to Chrissie, "if you don't want to stay for the rest of it, it's OK with me."

Chrissie gave her friend a quizzical look. "This has nothing to do with Ian Brown and Fiona Campbell being here, has it?

Maisie bent forward to pick up her handbag from the floor as the 'lovers' left their seats and headed to the theatre bar. She pulled Chrissie down beside her. "Don't let them see us," she hissed.

"I think they already have," Chrissie hissed back, catching Fiona pointing at them, from the corner of her eye.

Maisie cringed. "Don't look at them," she murmured, her agitation increasing by the minute. The couple moved on with the crowd.

"They're gone," Chrissie informed her, bemused at the change that had overtaken Maisie. Not the sophisticated young lady who'd suggested the theatre, but a shy child who'd been caught with her fingers in the biscuit tin. "You can come up now."

Maisie straightened and cautiously looked around.

"Let's go home," she pleaded. "I don't want to be here when THEY come back to their seats."

Chrissie looked around for another exit. "There," she said, "over there." A green neon 'exit' sign was lit above a curtain-covered door. Keeping low the two girls edged towards their escape route. Maisie felt like a criminal, sneaking away from the scene of a crime, but it was the only way out. She couldn't bear to see the look of smugness that would surely be all over Fiona Campbell's face and as for Ian Brown, she never wanted to see him again, EVER.

-----oOo-----

Chapter 18

The arrival of Chrissie, bearing gifts, lifted Maisie's spirits slightly.

"Happy Birthday," She trilled, plonking herself down on the pink velvet chair and waving a carefully wrapped package in front of her.

"For me?"

"Of course it's for you, Miss Seventeen."

Maisie smiled. Birthdays weren't celebrated much in the Green household, no birthday cake, nor cards nor 'pressies', just another day in fact.

Maisie opened her gift. A box of twenty assorted eye shadows, ranging from smoky brown to lurid blue looked back. Chrissie was her best friend and she almost cried with gratitude. Of all the people in the world who could have given her a birthday present, Chrissie was the only one.

"Thanks Chrissie," she said simply, "it's the best present I've ever had."

Chrissie beamed. "I'm glad you like it," she said, "and I thought you needed a bit of 'colour' in your life after that dreary play."

Maisie put the present aside. "You know it wasn't the dreary play that upset me, don't you."

Chrissie nodded. "I thought he liked you," she said, "Ian Brown, I mean."

"I know who you mean Chrissie," Maisie said, "just goes to show how wrong we were."

"Does that mean we won't be going back to the Badminton?"

"Don't know," said Maisie, shrugging, "don't think so," she added, feeling her dreams for the future disappear from her heart.

"Join the Club," said Chrissie, wistfully, "Tommy hasn't written either, so I guess we're going to be 'on the shelf' forever!"

Maisie gazed into the middle distance. She had been so keen to better herself, she hadn't thought things through, she may have a nicer bedroom and a new job as a Bonus Checker, she may have changed her looks and tried to like the theatre and badminton, but underneath it all, she still felt like Maisie Green from Fintry. 'Plenty more where you've come from', Shug Reilly had said at Keiller's Dance and Maisie felt he was right. She wasn't special at all, she wasn't a Fiona Campbell, she was just another girl from 'Wintry Fintry.'

Chrissie watched her friend become more crestfallen.

"Hey," she said, "penny for your thoughts."

Maisie looked at her. "I'm thinking," she said, "that I'm just a big, fat failure."

Chrissie looked shocked, as Maisie's eyes glistened with tears.

"NO YOU'RE NOT," she said stoutly, "why you're the bestest friend anyone could have and you're the prettiest girl in Keiller's and Ian Brown must be plain daft if he likes Fiona Campbell more than you."

Maisie responded with a mix of tears and laughter. "Oh, Chrissie," she said, "I'm so glad we're friends, I don't know what I'd do without you."

Chrissie pulled a handkerchief from her coat pocket. "Here," she said softly, "dry them eyes Maisie Green and get some of that birthday eye shadow on. Tonight we're going back to the Monkey Parade to find some more frogs to kiss and Tommy Murphy and Ian Brown and all the rest of them, can just go jump in the Swannie Ponds."

Ian Brown was woken up on Sunday morning by Rebel whining at his bedroom door. He looked at the clock. Eight thirty, well past his usual time for getting up and for Rebel's walk.

He threw back the covers and opened the bedroom door. Rebel bounced in, his tail wagging furiously.

"I'm glad someone likes me," he told his dog, as thoughts of being seen out with Fiona, by Maisie of all people, filled his troubled mind. He knew what she must have thought and was sure that Fiona would have lost no time in convincing Maisie that they were an item.

"C'mon boy," he said to Rebel, "let's have a walk and a think."

Ian pulled on his jeans and a thick jumper, work boots and a hooded parka. As soon as he stepped outside, he was glad that he had, a heavy frost had settled overnight and the air was freezing. Master and dog turned into Caird Park where Rebel was released from his lead and Ian watched as his animal companion ran off in a cloud of frosted breath. Ian began his walk around the perimeter of the park, the only sound being the frosty grass crunching beneath his feet. How simple it must be if you're a dog, he thought, they eat, sleep and mate without a care in the world while people........well, he found no answer for the hurt inside and he had no one to blame but himself.

What had possessed him to agree to Fiona's invite, he knew she would read more into it than he intended and now, now he'd really blown it with Maisie.

He whistled for Rebel, who came bounding towards him, full of the joys of Spring despite it being Winter. He fastened the chain round his neck and headed home to the emptiness of his flat and his heart.

True to her word, Chrissie called in at Maisie's that evening, determined they would both have some fun. Maisie too, had decided it was no use 'crying over spilt milk.' Ian Brown had made his choice and she just had to accept it. Maisie thought sixteen had been a tough year and it looked like seventeen wasn't going to be any better, but she decided to put the theatre and badminton behind her and face the future boldly, with Chrissie by her side.

"You'd better wrap up," Chrissie said, a pair of pink fur earmuffs balanced on her head and an enormous scarf wrapped around her neck. A pair of sheepskin mitts and suede ankle boots completed her ensemble. "It's bitter out there," she shivered moving into the warmth of the Green's lobby.

Maisie donned her only winter coat, accompanied by a woollen Arran hat, scarf and mitts. She had considered wearing her Stiletto heels but the thought of an ungainly tumble at the Monkey Parade changed her mind and she too pulled on her winter boots.

"Not exactly dolly birds are we," Maisie giggled, looking at herself in the dressing-table mirror, "I think the only thing we'll pull dressed like this, is the abominable snowman!"

It had been dark outside since about half past three and now the black sky was ablaze with twinkling stars and a frosty crescent moon hung almost directly above them as they waited for their bus into town.

"Do you think anyone will be there tonight" Chrissie asked, "anyone different that is?"

"You never know," said Maisie, "but anyway, different or not, we're not going to be fooled again by any man...right?"

"Right."

The Green Years

But, despite the cold weather, the boredom of Sunday had brought the young and foolish out in their droves and Maisie and Chrissie joined in the Monkey Parade with all the rest.

Kenny Wilson nudged Rab Skelly. "Look who's just turned up," he said, a tinge of excitement in his voice despite his outward show of indifference.

Rab glanced over to the other side of the Murraygate and nudged Kenny back. "Chrissie Dalton as well," he said thoughtfully, "I heard she'd been seeing some navy bloke, but he's obviously gone back to sea, and left her all alone."

Maisie's dismissal of Kenny, on more than one occasion, had originally dented his manly pride, but at the same time it seemed to make her more and more desirable.

"Let's cross the road," Kenny said, "casual-like and see how things are with the 'wenches'."

Rab flinched. He wished Kenny would stop trying to be the big man all the time, then maybe they'd get somewhere with the girls.

Within seconds of crossing over they had fallen in behind Maisie and Chrissie. "Going our way?" Kenny asked, already placing his arm around Maisie's shoulder.

"Hi Chrissie," said Rab, ignoring Kenny's chat-up line, "mind if I walk with you for a wee while?" Both girls stopped and stared at one another, each silently asking the other if this was a good idea.

It was Chrissie who broke the stalemate. "If you want, Rab Skelly," she said, "but only for a wee while mind." She shrugged her shoulders at Maisie indicating that Rab Skelly wasn't Tommy Murphy, but he was better than nothing.

Maisie got the message. Kenny Wilson wasn't Ian Brown but he would do as a substitute for love till THE ONE came along.

Kenny couldn't believe his luck. He linked Maisie's arm through his and guided her past Rab and Chrissie and away from their earshot.

"How've you been then Maisie?" he asked, keeping everything polite and neutral, "haven't seen you around for a while."

"Like you care?"

Kenny felt the first butterflies of panic in his stomach. He couldn't let her dump him again.

"Of course, I care," he said and actually meant it, "I've been trying to talk to you for weeks now but......

"I've been busy," Maisie interrupted.

"Right oh," said Kenny, "busy like....."

"Busy with my new job," Maisie announced proudly, "I've been promoted to Bonus Checker."

"Well" Kenny smiled, "Bonus Checker....that's pretty special, that is."

At the mention of the world 'special' Maisie visibly brightened.

"And I've been to the theatre and joined a badminton club," she added, getting into her stride, "but how about you Kenny, what have you been up to?"

Kenny fell silent. What had he been up to, absolutely nothing!

He felt his face redden as he searched for words that would show Maisie that he too was special.

"I've joined the T.A.." The lie was out and once voiced, couldn't be retracted.

Maisie stopped walking and turned to face him. "Territorial Army," she said incredulously, "seriously?"

"Aye," he confirmed, "me and Rab joined a couple o' weeks ago."

"And do you get a uniform and a gun and everything?" she asked. Kenny Wilson had suddenly risen in stature before her eyes.

"I'm impressed," Maisie said, "so if there's a nuclear attack, you'll know what to do?"

Kenny began to panic. "Not yet," he said, "that comes later after we learn about the guns."

His free hand covered Maisie's, "so how about I buy you a coke to celebrate you new job and my joining the T.A.

Maisie nodded in admiration. "I'd like that," she said.

"So would I," answered the new recruit. First thing Monday, he and Rab would join the T.A.

-----oOo-----

Chapter 19

"What happened to you last night then?" Chrissie asked as they sat on the bus into work, this accompanied with a nudge and an exaggerated wink.

"I could ask you the same question, Chrissie Dalton. You can walk with me just for a wee while," she mimicked.

"Rab saw my safely home," Chrissie said trying not to smile, "and that was all."

"Quite the gentleman now he's joined the T.A. then?" Maisie said.

Chrissie turned to look at Maisie, waiting for the punch-line.

"Joined the T.A.," she echoed, her voice an octave higher than normal.

"Him and Kenny," Maisie confirmed, "he told me last night."

"Rab never said anything to me then," Chrissie murmured, a bit miffed at Rab's secret life, kept a secret from her.

"Ask him yourself," Maisie said, "unless, Kenny's a liar........"

"Oh no," Maisie groaned. "Don't tell me...."

Maisie fumed for the rest of the journey into work.

As soon as Kenny got into work on Monday he headed straight for the men's toilets. He knew Rab always came in ten minutes early to have a smoke before starting his shift and he had to speak to him before Maisie did.

The Green Years

"Rab! Rab!" he shouted into the smoky atmosphere, "Are you in there?"

The sound of a toilet flushing and a cubicle door opening signalled that Rab had had his fag and was now ready to face the world. He'd had a good Sunday at the Monkey Walk and felt that Chrissie Dalton was at least wavering, if not completely convinced, of his feelings towards her.

"What's all the racket about?" he asked, spying Kenny half-way through the toilet door.

"We need to talk," Kenny said, "NOW."

Rab followed him out into the corridor.

The look of fear on Kenny's face couldn't be ignored and Rab fell into step alongside him as they headed to the Sugar Boiling Room.

"What's up?" Rab asked anxiously, "has some man caught you with his missus or something?"

Kenny pulled Rab closer. "It's worse than that," he said, "I told Maisie Green that you and me were in the T.A. and she was mighty impressed Rab, so we need to join, right, before she finds out that it was nonsense and she dumps me again."

"THE T.A." Rab said, incredulously, "you mean the 'Terries,' short haircuts and itchy uniforms and running around with toy guns?"

Kenny gritted his teeth. Rab wasn't going to be the pushover he'd imagined.

"Rab," he pleaded, "you should've seen the look of love on Maisie Green's face when I told her we'd joined up."

Rab's teeth were also gritted. "Will you stop saying WE. I've no' joined up and I don't intend to, so you're on your own pal."

"WAIT UP," Kenny called to Rab's disappearing back, "just think how much Chrissie will want you, she likes a man in uniform." Kenny watched the slowing of Rab's

113

steps as his words sank in. "That Navy bloke for instance, she really liked him," he added smoothly.

Rab turned, "do you think so?" Kenny knew he had won the argument and went in for the kill.

"Just picture it Rab," he said, now getting into the swing of things, "you and me, smart uniforms, men of the world protecting our women...particularly Maisie and Chrissie. What do you say, Rab, are you with me?"

Rab nodded slowly. "Let's do it," he said, warming to the picture that Kenny had painted, "it's in Rodd Road isn't it," he asked, "wherever that is."

"Don't worry about that," Kenny said, "Shug Reilly's in the T.A., he'll give us the low down at dinnertime. And remember Rab, we're already IN the T.A. so if Maisie or Chrissie ask anything, just make something up, right?"

Rab wasn't very good at 'making things up' not like Kenny who had the 'gift of the gab,' but agreed anyway and would be avoiding the girls like the plague till he had signed on the dotted line.

They gave the canteen a miss and went to Wallace's Pie Shop instead, eating their pies in the courtyard outside the factory while waiting for Shug to join the crowd of smokers.

"There he is!" exclaimed Kenny, as their workmate strolled out into the yard. "C'mon, let's go," he nudged Rab, who was fishing out a packet of ciggies and matches out of his pocket.

"Hey Shug," Kenny called out to him, "how's it going?"

Shug Reilly was no fool. If Kenny Wilson was seeking out his company there had to be a catch.

He eyed the two pals. "Ciggie?" offered Rab.

Shug took the 'bribe,' he was now sure they were after something.

"Thanks lads," he said, "things are going OK," he countered.

The Green Years

"Good, good," said Kenny, "nice to know."

Shug was now certain he was about to be 'tapped' for money.

"Before you ask," he said, "I'm skint, so if you're looking for a 'sub' then you'd better look elsewhere."

"NO, NO," Kenny assured him, "just being friendly like."

Shug lit the cigarette.

"Actually," Kenny shrugged, "me and Rab were thinking of joining the T.A., you know, the Terries and well......"

Shug's laughter echoed round the yard. "YOU TWO," he spluttered, "want to be soldiers!"

Kenny looked at Rab then back to Shug.

"What's so funny about that?"

"Well sonny, the T.A.'s for men, not BOYS."

"We're not boys," Kenny retorted, miffed at the suggestion, "I'll be 21 next birthday and Rab'll be 20, so we're hardly BOYS."

Shug raised his eyebrows and drew deeply on the cigarette.

Might be the making of them, he thought, and the other lads would soon show them the difference between MEN and BOYS, especially at square bashing.

He dropped the last of his cigarette and crushed it underfoot.

"Alright," he said, "if you're serious, we train every Wednesday night, so if you want to see what it's all about, I'll see you then."

With that Shug Reilly shook his head and began walking away.

"If you're man enough," he called over his shoulder, grinning.

It was Rab who spoke first. "I don't think this is a good idea Kenny," he said quietly, "can you not just tell Maisie the truth...."

"Not an option," said Kenny, quickly making up his mind that he was going to join the T.A. with or without Rab. He had seen the look on Maisie's face and wanted her more than ever.

Maisie and Chrissie ate their dinner in silence, each wondering if Kenny was lying or Rab was secretive.

"Is there still no sign of them?" Maisie asked, glancing round the canteen.

"Nope."

"Trying to avoid us I'll bet," said Maisie, "in case we ask them about the T.A."

The hands of the clock moved towards the end of dinner-time.

"Well," Maisie said resignation heavy on her shoulders, "looks like we've been fooled by a man again." She pushed back her chair, resignation moving into annoyance.

"Let's get back to the toil," she said to Chrissie, "and I think we should go back to the Badminton," she added determinedly, "no man is going to stop me doing anything I want ever again, even Ian Brown."

Chrissie quickly agreed. She'd liked playing Badminton and despite having warmed to Rab's attention on Sunday, she too was determined to have fun without men.

-----oOo-----

Chapter 20

Kenny and Rab had managed to avoid the girls by 'dining out' at dinnertime and avoiding the canteen at tea breaks, making do with a fag and Mars Bar instead.

"This is getting daft," Rab moaned, "it's freezin' out here, can we no' sneak into the canteen for a cup o' tea at least?"

"This is the last day we'll have to do this," Kenny reminded him, "and thanks for changing your mind about joining. You're a real pal."

Rab zipped up his leather jacket and cupped his frozen hands round the glow of his cigarette.

"It'd better be worth it," he said. "The things I do for the love of women!" he added, giving Kenny his martyred look, "and if this doesn't swing it for Chrissie, I'll be out o' the T.A. before you can say 'quick march.'"

"C'mon big man," Kenny responded, encouragingly, "let's join first before you start talking about leaving."

At half past seven that evening, the two lads made their way to the T.A. H.Q. at Rodd Road.

"This looks like a REAL army base," Rab whispered, "are you sure we can leave if we want to?"

"Stop worrying," Kenny said, "just follow me and you'll be OK."

They walked towards the gate in the fence that surrounded the complex but were halted in their tracks by a uniformed squaddie, complete with rifle, which Rab hoped was made of wood and not real.

"What's your business?" the squaddie asked.

"We want to join the T.A." Kenny said smartly, "a mate of ours, Shug Reilly said we could join tonight."

The soldier stepped back. "Did he now?" he stated with a hint of menace in his voice. "What was his name again?"

"Reilly, Rab said, "Shug Reilly......I mean, Hugh Reilly."

"Hugh Reilly," the soldier mused, stroking his chin in thought, "mmmmhhhh, I think I remember something about two yobs expected tonight. Would that be you two?"

Kenny and Rab glanced at each other. "YOBS," Rab mouthed.

Kenny nudged him, "that's right," he agreed, "that'll be us."

The soldier nodded towards the door of a large building in the middle of the base. "Over there," he said, openly smirking "and by the way...." he added, "you'd better get your hair cut, or your head'll be too big for your T.A. hat."

"HAIR CUT," Rab visibly flinched. He was very proud of his Tony Curtis hairstyle.

"You didn't say we'd have to get our hair cut," he hissed to Kenny as he followed him through the gate, "I've changed my mind Kenny," he gasped, "I'm no' joining."

"Get a grip Rab," Kenny instructed, pulling him nearer to the door of the building, "you can always grow it again when you leave."

Kenny knew if he let go of Rab's arm, he'd make a run for it. His grip tightened as they went through the door. The interior was a huge drill hall, where an Instructor was putting some lads through their paces. An officer sat at a desk by the door and stood up when Kenny and Rab entered.

The Green Years

"What's your business lads?" he asked, casting an experienced eye over the teddy-boy suits and beetle-crusher shoes.

"We want to join......sir," said Kenny, pointing to Rab and himself, "the T.A. that is."

"Well," said the officer, "you've come to the right place."

He indicated two metal chairs set against the wall of the drill hall. "Pull up a pew and tell me a bit about yourselves."

For the next half hour, Kenny and Rab, but mainly Kenny, told their life stories, their schools, their jobs and their reasons for wanting to be a soldier.

"Well," he concluded, "I think you're just what the T.A. is looking for." Kenny beamed and Rab glowered.

He produced some forms and pens. "Fill these in and I'll let you know when and where for your medical and training dates as soon as they're processed."

The boys scribbled silently till the forms were completed.

"Is that it?" asked Kenny, handing them over to the officer.

"That's it," he said, standing up to let them know the interview was over. He shook hands with both of them.

"Welcome to the T.A." he smiled and we'll be in touch.

Once outside, Rab began again to question the wisdom of his decision.

"Stop fretting," said Kenny, "you're getting to sound like an auld fish wifie. Everything will be OK, so cheer up and when Chrissie and Maisie see us in our uniforms, you'll realise I was right."

The squaddie was still on duty at the gate but he'd been joined by a familiar figure.

"Lads!" said the uniformed Shug Reilly, "so you came after all."

He shook both their hands.

Sandra Savage

"Didn't think you'd have the bottle," he continued, "but here you are and as new recruits you'll be under the gentle wing of a Sergeant till you know the ropes and.........." he added, gleefully, "that would be me."

He pointed to the three chevron stripes on the sleeve of his jacket. "See you soon," he added, as he turned to go, "and I'm looking forward to it already."

A slight shimmer of anxiety ran through Rab's stomach.

Shug Reilly was a bit of a hard man and being under his gentle wing didn't do anything to inspire his confidence.

Rab fretted inwardly all the way back to Fintry, as he tried to think of a way to backtrack his decision without looking stupid in the eyes of Kenny.

"See you tomorrow at Keiller's," Kenny said as they alighted from their bus, "and thanks, pal," he added "for, well being a pal."

He slapped Rab on the back and walked away, leaving the reluctant squaddie alone with his anxiety.

The next day in the canteen, Kenny lost no time in approaching Maisie and Chrissie.

"How goes it girls?" he asked grinning with confidence.

Maisie's eyes levelled with his. "Does the word LIAR mean anything to you Kenny Wilson?" she hissed.

"ME," Kenny retorted, "are you talking about ME?"

Maisie looked around her. "Well I don't see anyone else at this table!"

Chrissie joined in the confrontation. "You and Rab haven't joined the T.A. at all, have you?"

Kenny turned his attention to his accuser.

"If Rab had joined the T.A. he would have told me last Sunday at the Monkey Parade and he didn't say a word," Chrissie stated confidently.

"Maybe he doesn't trust you," Kenny retaliated, "to tell you things."

The Green Years

The comment stung Chrissie's heart, already damaged by Tommy Murphy and she pushed her chair back and stood up.

"Well then," she said, pointing out Rab at another table, "bring him over here and let him tell me now."

Rab had been watching the altercation from afar and when Kenny signalled him to join them, he knew it meant trouble.

"What's up?" he asked as casually as he could.

"Have you and HIM, joined the T.A. or not?" Chrissie asked.

Kenny stood with arms folded, avoiding any eye contact with Rab. He knew the score. Rab wouldn't let him down.

He was up the Clyde without a paddle and Rab knew it.

Back Kenny and lose Chrissie. Or back Chrissie and lose the respect of his pal.

"Who told you we'd joined the T.A.?"

Chrissie looked at Maisie. "I did," she said, "and HE told me last Sunday at the Monkey Walk." All eyes turned to Kenny, whose mind was racing at a hundred miles an hour searching for a way out of his predicament without losing face.

"And we HAVE joined the T.A.," he said slowly, "only I joined a couple of weeks ago and Rab just joined last night."

He put his arm round Rab's shoulder. "Isn't that right, pal?"

"Right," Rab agreed, anxiously, looking at Chrissie for understanding.

"I was going to surprise you in my uniform," he told her, compounding the lie. He'd have to stick to his guns now as Chrissie's eyes changed from anger to the beginnings of admiration.

"So, you hadn't joined till last night?" she asked.

Rab's breathing began to normalise. "That's right Chrissie," he said, "I would have told you if I'd joined before that."

Both girls seemed to relax as the bell for the end of teabreak sounded.

"So, will we see you later?" Kenny asked, falling in step with Maisie. "You might," she said, "feeling vindicated in Chrissie's eyes, "maybe we could go to the pictures, or something," she added coyly.

Kenny was elated. "I'll check things out in the Courier and see what's on."

"And maybe Rab and Chrissie would like to come too, make it a foursome," she said, now confident that she could ask anything of her 'budding soldier' and he'd agree.

This wasn't quite how Kenny had wanted their date to be, but at least he was making progress.

"Great," he said smiling, and winking at Rab, "the four of us."

The girls returned to the Packing Department with suppressed smiles.

"I think we might have Kenny and Rab where we want them," Maisie whispered, "isn't life FUN?"

"FUN," Chrissie echoed, but she was beginning to like Rab and wasn't sure how far Maisie meant to go in her pursuit of FUN.

-----oOo-----

Chapter 21

Ian Brown had been fretting since that evening at the Rep and Fiona had been unbearably fawning. He'd prayed that Maisie would turn up again at the Badminton, but there had been no sign of her the week before and he doubted if he'd ever see her again.

"Penny for them?" Fiona chirped, sitting herself down beside Ian in the Church Hall. Badminton night again and she couldn't wait.

Ian continued to bounce his Badminton racket against his other hand and barely looked up.

Fiona was irritated at his lack of response. She had thought that after their night out together at the theatre, that he'd be a bit more daring and now that Maisie Green was out of the way, she'd done everything to encourage his attentions.

"Not worth a penny," he said standing up and taking a shuttlecock from the box. Fiona followed him.

"Ready to start?" she asked, brightly, taking up her position on the opposite side of the net.

The rest of the players gradually drifted in and waved to the pair of them, nudging occasionally and smiling.

"She's got her claws into him now," one of the girls said to her partner.

"About time," came the reply, "she's been after him for ages."

Maisie and Chrissie sidled into the hall just after eight o'clock.

"Told you we'd be too late," whispered Chrissie, "all the courts are full."

"Sorry," said Maisie, trying not to look for Ian Brown amongst the moving bodies, "I had to work late with Ella, one of the Packers bonuses was wrong and she wouldn't quit till we'd got it right."

"I know," said Chrissie changing her shoes," maybe someone will be finishing soon."

Ian Brown and Fiona Campbell shook hands over the net and started moving towards the girls. Maisie felt herself flush with embarrassment and wanted to run out of the hall and as far away as possible from the cosy pair.

"Maisie!" exclaimed Ian Brown, finally looking up and spotting her.

"You're here," he added his whole face lighting up while Fiona's darkened.

Fiona linked her arm into Ian's and smiled possessively at Maisie.

"Nice to see you both again," she smoothed, "Ian and I were wondering where you'd got to."

Maisie felt herself bristle, but Chrissie's hand on her shoulder was holding her down.

"Is that the court free now?" Chrissie asked.

Fiona gazed at Ian. "Is it free?" she said airily, "have we had enough fun for one night, or do you want some more?"

"I think some more," Ian grinned, taking Maisie by the hand and propelling her towards the empty court, "never can get enough of a good thing," he added, locking his eyes on Maisie's.

Chrissie jumped in before Fiona could say another word.

"You and me then," she beamed, "and may the best woman win."

The Green Years

The words weren't lost on Fiona as she fumed after Chrissie onto the next court.

Ian Brown couldn't believe his luck. Now he had Maisie's attention again, he'd be able to explain to her about Fiona meaning nothing to him and ask her for a date.

Maisie was useless at Badminton and was glad when Ian called a halt to their game and led her to the table with the Orange Squash and tumblers.

"Here," he said, handing her a glass of the cold juice, "you're getting better at the game and next time, I'll show you some shots."

"Next time," Maisie queried, gulping down the cooling drink,

"I doubt if there'll be a next time," she said, remembering how rejected she'd felt on seeing him with Fiona at the theatre. "I don't think Badminton is for me."

Ian felt his good mood go from exuberant to dejected in a split second.

"But, you're only learning," he rushed, "you'll get better."

Fiona was approaching rapidly, with Chrissie in her wake, but Maisie couldn't bear to watch another example of their togetherness.

"Well here's your girlfriend," she said quickly standing and joining Chrissie. "Our boyfriends are meeting us for a drink later and we don't want to keep them waiting, do we Chrissie?"

"Boyfriends," Ian said weakly.

"Yes," Maisie repeated, "they're soldiers in the T.A. and they finish gun practice at nine."

Chrissie looked bemused. What was Maisie on about?

"So," she said with a superior nod as she handed her racket to Fiona, "we don't want to keep the boys waiting, do we!"

Once out in the cold air, Chrissie pulled Maisie to a stop.

"What was all that about?" she said, squeakily, "we're not meeting Kenny and Rab......"

"WE know that," said Maisie, "but Mr Brown and Miss Smartypants don't."

"C'mon," Maisie said, "let's go home and leave the lovebirds to themselves."

"But, I thought you liked Ian Brown?" Chrissie asked, more confused than usual about Maisie's romantic swings and roundabouts.

"USED TO," Maisie emphasised, "used to like Ian Brown, but I'm not about to go into a competition for him. If he likes me, then he's going to have to chase me," she said with finality, "and I'm getting harder to catch."

Chrissie sighed. "So Kenny's the hot favourite now is he?"

"At the moment," Maisie said airily, "but who knows."

Chrissie was beginning to get concerned about Maisie's thinking about the men in her life. They'd hurt her in the past, that was for sure, but the way she was behaving now, wasn't like her at all.

The bravado Maisie had felt at the Badminton Club, dissipated as she said goodbye to Chrissie and made her way back home.

She'd tried to be unconcerned that Ian Brown and Fiona Campbell were now an 'item' but her pride wouldn't let it show and she knew that she could never fit into their world and nor did she want to, she told herself decisively, as she turned her key in the lock of home and went inside.

Ian Brown packed away his things in silence. Maisie had a boyfriend, the words dug into his chest and a soldier too, who knew how to handle guns. His job as a security guard and dog handler suddenly seemed pathetic against the charisma of a soldier.

The Green Years

"Alright Ian?" Fiona asked, glad that Maisie Green now had a boyfriend of her own, but annoyed at Ian's sullen silence.

She was here for him wasn't she? Maisie Green didn't come up to her knee caps for style, so what was his problem?

"Fancy coming back for a coffee or something?" Fiona suggested, "we've got a fancy new coffee pot...."

But the dismal look on Ian's face made her drop the subject.

She was getting annoyed again. What did she have to do to make him love her?

Exasperated, she threw on her jacket and headed for the door.

"See you next week," she called as she left the hall. But Ian Brown wasn't listening,

-----oOo-----

Sandra Savage

Chapter 22

The next day at work, there was an envelope on Chrissie's packing table with Maisie's name on it.

"It was there when I clocked on," she said, excitedly, as they waited in line for their turn at the tea urn, "hurry up and open it."

"In a minute," Maisie said, struggling for change from her purse, "I want to get a couple of scones first."

Finally, they were at their table, tea and scones scoffed, before Maisie opened the envelope.

Dear Maisie and Chrissie, it read, Rab and me want to know if you'll come to the pictures with us on Thursday night. Psycho is on at the Broadway and we'll meet you there at seven o'clock if that's alright? Wave if you agree. Kenny

Maisie looked up. "Do you want to go to the pictures with Rab and Kenny on Thursday?" she asked Chrissie.

"Is that what the note's all about?"

Maisie nodded. And we've to wave to Kenny if we decide to go.

Chrissie turned and beamed a smile at Rab and his heart went into overdrive.

Maisie waved, queen-like to Kenny.

"They're coming," Kenny murmured to the smitten Rab as he waved back, "we've cracked it."

"And you think this is all because we've joined the T.A.? Rab asked in disbelief.

The Green Years

"I do," said Kenny knowledgably, "girls love a man in uniform," he said, "it's a known fact. And speaking of the T.A.," Kenny said lowering his voice, "maybe if we got our haircut before Thursday, the girls would know for sure we meant business."

Rab's hand flew automatically to his Elvis quiff. "HAIRCUT," he breathed through gritted teeth, "do you really think we need to go that far?"

Kenny sighed, "Rab my man," he said patiently, "you heard the squaddie about needing to get a haircut so we may as well kill two birds with one stone, so to speak. How about it?"

Rab felt boxed into a corner. "If you're sure," he agreed, unsteadily, "really sure."

"Never surer," Kenny told him, "so after work we'll stop in at Tony's up the Overgate, for a 'short back and sides.'"

With great misgivings on the part of Rab, the boys entered the barber's shop.

"Hey lads," smiled the proprietor, casting his professional eye over the two teddy boys. "What's you like today, huh?" he asked in his broken Italian accent.

Kenny pushed Rab forward before he made a break for it.

"Short back and sides," he said, "twice" he added pointing at Rab and then himself.

Tony's eyebrows lifted as his eyes widened in surprise, but he wasn't one to argue with two teddy boys.

"Fine choice," he said, ushering Rab to the barber's chair and draping a large white towel over his chest.

For the next 15 minutes the only sound was the scissors cutting off Rab's treasured locks and the buzz of the clippers finishing the job. Rab had kept his eyes lowered the whole time but eventually he looked up at himself in the mirror.

Who was this man with the big ears and white neck who stared back at him. He looked at Kenny, the pain of loss evident in his eyes.

"You look just like a real soldier now," Kenny said unconvincingly, as he took his turn in the chair.

"Same again," he told Tony, "we've joined the T.A.," he added "and they don't go in for fancy haircuts."

Tony nodded wisely.

"T.A.", he said almost reverently, "what's that?"

"Territorial Army," said Kenny, "you know, incase there's a nuclear war and stuff."

Even Rab was impressed when Kenny put it like that.

"I see," the barber said, thoughtfully, "long hair might catch on fire in nuclear war, right?"

"Right," said Kenny, nodding at the shorn Rab, "don't want burnt hair, do we?"

Even Kenny felt the chill of the night air on his neck as the lads made their way home.

"It'll be worth it," he kept telling the unhappy Rab "and when we get our uniforms......" Kenny's imagination pictured the sight, "the girls will be putty in our hands."

Thursday night came around and Chrissie spent a long time perfecting her look. She was seeing Rab with new eyes now and couldn't wait to meet up with him at the cinema. Tommy Murphy hadn't bothered to even send her a postcard, but now it had stopped bothering her. She'd even taken off the silver bracelet he'd bought her and put it in her dressing table drawer out of sight.

"You look nice," Mrs Dalton said, glad to see that Chrissie was getting back to normal after the distress she'd suffered with the departure of Tommy Murphy.

"We're going to the pictures," she said happily, unable to keep the smile off her face.

"We?"

The Green Years

"It's a foursome," Chrissie said, "me and Maisie and two of the lads from Keiller's."

"No names?"

"If you must know," Chrissie said, "his name's Rab, Rab Skelly."

"Do we know him?"

"Questions, questions," Chrissie replied, "we're just going to the Broadway Cinema in Arthurstone Terrace and that's not anywhere near Forfar."

The barb hit home.

"We didn't know where you were?" Grace Dalton said anxiously, not wanting to have a rerun of that unhappy event.

Chrissie bent to kiss her mother on the cheek.

"Well, that's all over now," she said feeling very grown up, "so stop worrying."

Maisie wasn't sure about any of it.

She'd engineered the whole thing but for all the wrong reasons.

Why was it that the ones you liked didn't like you, she surmised and the ones you couldn't care less about stuck to you like glue? And even as she said it, she felt ashamed. Kenny Wilson could have any girl in Keiller's but he had asked her out, so why was she not delighted? She made the minimum effort in getting ready for the date and her mind kept wandering back to the Badminton Hall and Ian Brown. Why had he chosen Fiona over her? But the answer she knew already, Fiona had class.

She pulled on her coat and headed out to meet Chrissie and the lads at the cinema. After all, it was a free night out and she might even enjoy it.

Rab and Kenny had agreed their usual attire of drainpipe trousers and beetle-crusher shoes weren't going to work with their new haircuts.

"Jeans and a thick jumper," Kenny had advised, "preferably one that came up to the ears."

All three of the foursome were waiting outside the cinema when Maisie arrived. "Hurry up," signalled Chrissie, "it's freezing out here."

Maisie quickened her step and hurried into the cinema behind the rest. It took her a second look to realise what was different about her beau.

"Your hair," she said incredulously, looking from one lad to the other, "it's........it's so short."

Rab bristled and Kenny nodded. "Long hair and the T.A. don't mix," he advised her, tapping the side of his nose knowingly.

"I like it," Chrissie said, smiling at her big-eared date, "I think it's, well, manly."

She couldn't have chosen a better word to describe Rab's hair if she'd tried, and he straightened up instantly, running his fingers through the sparse crop. Kenny had been right all along.

Maisie kept giving Kenny sidelong glances in the darkness of the cinema. After all, she had cropped her own hair to change her image, so why couldn't Kenny. His arm draped itself around her shoulder and tightened when a scary bit in the movie made Maisie jump.

"Nothing to be scared of," he whispered, "not with me around."

And, surprisingly, for the first time in a long time, Maisie felt quite safe under the protection of a man.

-----oOo-----

Chapter 23

It was the last Saturday before Christmas when Chrissie came knocking at Maisie's door.

"Where's the fire?" asked Maisie as her friend pushed past her into the house, waving an airmail envelope in her hand.

Maisie followed Chrissie into her bedroom. She'd never seen Chrissie so rattled before. "What's up?" she asked anxiously, closing the bedroom door behind her.

"This," murmured Chrissie, thrusting the envelope into Maisie's hand. "Just when I'd gotten over him and decided Rab was the man for me........THIS."

Maisie opened the envelope and two sheets of airmail paper slipped out.

Dearest Chrissie, it said, I know it's been a while, but I've been at sea for weeks and only just docked at Suez long enough to post this letter to you. I know I'm the last person you want to hear from, but please, please forgive me. I don't know why I ran away, I just felt scared and well, your mum and dad were really angry.

If you still think of me at all, I will be back in Dundee at New Year and would ask you to meet me again like before, at the dock gates at 11 o'clock in the morning on New Year's Eve.

I'll understand if you don't come, but please think about it.

Do you still wear your bracelet. I hope so. Love, Tommy.

Maisie folded the pages and returned them to the envelope.

"Well?" she asked?

Chrissie raised her shoulders in resignation. "Well what?" she whispered.

"Well what are you going to do about Tommy Murphy?"

Chrissie shook her head. "Don't know."

Maisie took a deep breath. "Do you love him?" she asked quietly, "I mean, really love him?"

Tears began to trickle down Chrissie's cheeks. "I thought I did," she mumbled, "but now that me and Rab are getting on so well.....I don't know any more."

Maisie sat down beside Chrissie and put her arm around her shoulder. "If you're not sure Chrisse," she counselled, "then maybe you shouldn't settle for either of them."

Two worried blue eyes looked at Maisie. "Then I might lose both of them and end up on the shelf. I'm not pretty like you Maisie, you can pick and choose, but me......"

"Don't be daft," Maisie said, surprised that Chrissie should think such a thing, "remember about kissing frogs," she smiled, "maybe you just need to kiss a few more."

"Not funny," said Chrissie sadly.

Maisie handed her a paper tissue from her handbag before producing a coin from her purse.

"We'll toss for it," Maisie said, "heads it's Rab, tails it's Tommy."

Chrissie's eyes widened, "and what if it doesn't come down the right way," she said, "what if its heads for Rab but I want Tommy or the other way about?"

"Aahaa," said Maisie, that's the trick. Depending on how the coin falls will tell you how you really feel about them."

Maisie prepared to flip the coin, "Heads it's Rab, Tails Tommy's the one, Ready?" she asked.

Chrissie's eyes got wider as she watched the coin spin into the air before landing on the lino and rolling under the bed.

"Move your feet," she said to Chrissie, "I'll get it."

"I think it's heads," said Maisie "Rab wins." She watched Chrissie's reaction. "Is it?" she said unenthusiastically. "No," Maisie corrected, I got that wrong, it's tails, its Tommy."

The reaction was unmistakable. Chrissie's eyes lit up and a smile flickered at her lips. "Really?" she breathed.

"Really," Maisie agreed. "So the coin has decided for you, it's Tommy you really want."

But almost instantly, uncertainty swept in. "But what if he doesn't really love me," Chrissie said, a frown returning to her face "and he runs away again?"

Maisie returned the coin to her purse, "that's the chance we all take Chrissie," she said, more to herself than to her friend, "real life isn't like the movies with its 'happy ever after' in fact it isn't like the movies at all," she concluded profoundly. "Sometimes love just hurts."

The girls gazed at nothing in particular as the realisation that things don't always work out as you want sank in, especially things that involved boys. Maisie's affections for Kenny had bounced between love and hate for months now and although she was now leaning towards trusting him again, just a little bit, her thoughts constantly wandered to the figure of Ian Brown at the Badminton Club. What did Fiona have that she didn't?

"Penny for them?" Chrissie said, interrupting Maisie's reverie of Ian Brown. "I was just thinking," said Maisie, "it's time we stopped worrying about being left on the shelf and try a bit harder at not getting hurt."

When Chrissie had gone, Maisie took the coin out of her purse again. "Heads its Kenny," she said aloud, "tails its Ian." She tossed the coin. Tails. She put the coin back into her purse. Fiona Campbell had better watch out.

Kenny and Rab were getting used to their T.A. haircuts and the effect they were having on the girls, when their letters arrived ordering them to report to the Territorial Army Camp at Barry Buddon for their initial week's training.

"This is it," said Kenny sharply, "we're going to be fully trained and kitted out for the New Year and when we turn up at the City Square with Maisie and Chrissie to kiss the auld year cheerio, we'll be kissing the girls hello!"

He slapped Rab on the back. "Was I right," he said grinning, "or was I right!"

Rab conceded, "you were right Kenny," he said, "as usual."

The T.A. had cleared things with Keiller's for the boys to have the time off and a late winter sun also showed its face, along with Maisie and Chrissie, as they boarded the bus at the Seagate to take them to the camp.

"See you in a week then," Kenny said beginning to regret the idea of Maisie seeing him off. After all, they were only going a few miles up the road to Barry Buddon, not out to a war zone.

But Maisie played along. "A week it is," she said smiling "and will you have on your uniform when you come back?" she asked, quite looking forward to seeing him in full battle-dress.

He looked at Rab. "What do you reckon," he said, "kit and caboodle?"

Rab nodded, conscious of Chrissie standing beside him and not sure whether to kiss her goodbye or shake her hand.

But the bus driver made the decision for him. "Hurry up and give her a kiss mate, this bus is for leaving."

Chrissie felt her face go scarlet and Rab leant down and kissed her cheek. "See you in a week?" he asked, unsure if she would still fancy him a week from now. Chrissie nodded and quickly stepped back, the letter from Tommy sitting darkly in her clutch bag.

The girls waved as the bus backed out of the bus station carrying Kenny and Rab into the unknown of Barry Buddon T.A. Camp. "Do you think they'll wait for us?" Rab asked anxiously.

"We're only going to be away a week Rab," Kenny reassured him, "and if they're not," he added, glibly, "there's plenty more pebbles on the beach and in our army gear, we'll have our pick."

But as the bus picked up speed and headed out along the Broughty Ferry Road towards Barry Buddon, Kenny realised that his blasé front was just that, a front, for deep inside he now knew for certain, Maisie was the one.

Kenny and Rab were amongst eight others who were reporting for duty that day and Shug Reilly was there to meet them all.

"My name is Sergeant Reilly," he said, menacingly, "but you can call me SIR." Rab visibly jumped and even Kenny flinched at the word SIR.

"Get him," murmured Rab out of the corner of his mouth, just loud enough for Sergeant Reilly to hear.

"Did you have something to say to me son,'?" he asked Rab sweetly. Rab shook his head. "I didn't quite hear you?" the Sergeant said, cupping his hand around his ear.

"No," said Rab, his stomach now tightening. He'd always been a bit wary of Shug Reilly, but now he was proper scared, as Shug's face closed in on his.

"NO WHAT, SOLDIER?" he said.

Rab's mouth refused to move as did everyone else's, as they waited for the next word.

"SIR" blasted the Sergeant, "that's the word you're looking for son, SIR." Sergeant Reilly walked down the line before returning to Rab.

"Now," he said, his voice sweetness and light again, "I'll ask you again and this time, I want the correct response."

"Do you have something to say to me, son?"

Rab's face was white as he fought to untie the knot of fear in his stomach. "No, sir," he said. "LOUDER," barked the Sergeant.

"NO, SIR," Rab repeated, wishing the ground would open up and swallow him.

Satisfied, Shug Reilly resumed his position in front of the new recruits. "Follow me," he ordered, "and try to keep in line," this remarked directed specifically at Rab.

For the rest of the day, the recruits were issued with their kit and shown their bunks. "We eat at 6.30 sharp," ordered the Sergeant, "the Mess Hall is there," he told them, pointing in a vague direction, "don't be late."

Rab and Kenny sank down onto their bunks. The week was going to be harder than either of them had imagined, with Rab already thinking that no woman was worth this aggro, not even Chrissie.

Kenny could see the panic in Rab's eyes. A full week of this would either make or break him. "C'mon pal," he said, "let's find the Mess before all the grub's gone."

"I'm no' very hungry," said Rab, his stomach still knotted.

Kenny felt a twinge of conscience at how he'd steamrollered Rab into joining the T.A.

"Just let's give it a try," he said quietly, "we're here for the week so might as well at least enjoy the food."

Rab relented and stood up, following Kenny to the billet door.

"If we last a week," he muttered. Kenny put his hand on his shoulder. "We'll be OK," he said, more calmly than he felt, "just keep thinking of the New Year and the girls."

-----oOo-----

Chapter 24

Ian Brown was miserable as he walked with Rebel around the grounds of the National Cash Register Company, checking that all doors and windows were secure. The night air was frosty and Rebel's breathing left him in misty clouds.

What had gone wrong, he asked himself, time and again, without answer. He knew Maisie liked him, but the fates seemed to conspire against him every time he tried to get closer to her. And now, there was this 'boyfriend' of hers to contend with, the soldier.

Just then, Rebel barked and began to pull Ian towards the perimeter fence. "OK boy," Ian whispered, flashing his torch in the direction Rebel was pointing, all his senses alert now knowing that something was wrong. He unleashed Rebel who went hurtling into the darkness, while Ian ran behind him.

"Freeze," he shouted as a flurry of legs and arms tried to scramble under the wire fence, but Rebel had an arm in his grip and had no intention of letting go. Ian grabbed a leg and pulled a second intruder back into the compound.

"Get the doag aff me," a panicking voice screamed at Ian.

"Stop struggling," Ian shouted as he clamped a pair of handcuffs onto the other figure who was now lying face down in the grass.

The Green Years

"Release," he commanded Rebel who immediately dropped the intruder's arm but continued to stand over him.

"On your feet," Ian ordered, "the pair of you."

The trio staggered back to the Guardroom where the other guard was having a cuppa and reading the football results in his Sporting Post, oblivious to the drama.

"Phone Bell Street," Ian said sharply, annoyed at his colleague's laxity, "these two were trying to break in through the perimeter fence, but their luck was out this time," he added, "Rebel spotted them."

The phone call was made and Ian pulled off the balaclavas covering the intruders' faces.

"What the....." two pairs of sleekit eyes blinked in the brightness of the strip lights. The pair looked familiar, but Ian couldn't place them.

"How old are you two? Ian asked. The men looked at one another, "he's 17," one muttered, "I'm his big brother."

Ian shook his head. Losers. The police turned up within minutes.

"What's all this then?" one of them asked Ian.

"Caught them trying to break in through the perimeter fence, but Rebel and me were too quick for them."

"Don't I know you?" the other pc said, tipping up the older man's head to have a closer look.

"It's Ronnie Reid isn't it?"

"So whut if it is?" grunted the man, pulling his face away.

The pc turned to Ian. "You've done the police a favour, mate," he said, smiling "we've been trying to catch these two for a while now, but they've always managed to dodge us, but not this time, eh Ronnie," he concluded, "and wee Johnny too," he added, "what a bargain."

"See you in court," the pc said to Ian, handing back Ian's handcuffs and replacing them with their own, "and thanks again."

The next day the Courier carried the story.

HAVE A GO HERO SAVES NCR screamed the headline.

"Ian Brown and his faithful dog Rebel, last night single-handedly captured two known thieves as they tried to break into the grounds of the National Cash Register Company.

It's Rebel who's the hero, said Mr Brown and I'm just pleased that we managed to hold on to them till the police arrived.

The company has given Mr Brown three days paid leave in appreciation of his heroic action and devotion to duty and Rebel was rewarded with a juicy bone."

Pictures of Ian holding Rebel's paw and the two culprits being transferred to the cells by the police were splashed all over the page.

"Just doing my duty," he told Fiona when she called in at his flat on Clepington Road, waving the Courier. The last person he wanted to see was Fiona, but the more he tried to dissuade her, the more determined she seemed to become.

"DUTY!" echoed Fiona. "Don't be so modest, Ian, why it's the bravest thing I've ever heard of and I'm so proud of you."

She blew him a kiss. "That's for being wonderful," she added "and mum and dad have asked if you'd like to come to Sunday Lunch tomorrow, as a bit of a celebration........what do you think?"

As usual, he felt boxed in by Fiona's persistence. "Sorry," he murmured, "I've got some unexpected leave, so me and Rebel are taking off to the hills tomorrow....get some exercise," he finished lamely.

"But, it's the middle of winter," Fiona countered loudly, "you can't go out on the hills in this weather!"

Ian was beginning to wish he'd never met Fiona and her pushy ways. "Look," he said, guiding her towards the door, "thanks for the offer, but I really need some time away from this publicity nonsense, so if you could offer my apologies to your parents, that would really be appreciated..."

Fiona was silent, as she tried to think of something else to say that would prolong her stay in Ian's company, but her wits had deserted her.

"Thanks for coming round," Ian said, opening the door wider and pulling Rebel closer to him "maybe see you at the Badminton if I'm back by then."

Ian closed the door behind her with a sign of relief. He really needed to do something about Fiona. He knew how she felt about him and that her parents were secretly hoping that the two of them would 'get together,' but although they were a match financially and intellectually, there was nothing happening in his heart.

That place had already been filled by Maisie.

Sunday dawned, frosty and bitterly cold. Fiona had been right, there was no way he would take himself and Rebel onto the hills today, but at least he'd managed to avoid the Sunday lunch.

"C'mon Rebel," he said, stroking the dog's ears, "let's at least give you a nice long walk along the beach at Broughty." He loaded Rebel into the car and headed East towards the Ferry sands. There was no frost on the beach and Rebel plunged again and again into the water to retrieve the ball Ian had brought with him. "Race you to the car," he called out as he ran up the beach to the road with Rebel in hot pursuit. The sound of gunfire startled both dog and man. It was coming from close by and Ian quickly realised it was the sound of rifles being fired at the T.A. training camp at Barry Buddon.

Pictures of uniformed men with their weapons firing at the targets filled his head. Maisie's boyfriend might be there learning to fight like a man while he.... he was the 'have a go hero.' Pathetic. Once more he felt his spirits fall, as he realised that Fiona and her parents were probably right and he should settle for Fiona. He would never be man enough for Maisie Green.

But Maisie had also read the story of Ian's heroics in the Courier. "Isn't he brave," she breathed to Chrissie, as they pored over the newspaper in Chrissie's mother's kitchen.

"Who's brave?" asked Mrs Dalton, coming into the room with a basket of washing she'd just retrieved from the clothesline.

Maisie showed her the newspaper. She was about to tell her about the Den o' Mains episode, but realised in time, that Chrissie hadn't told her mother about their scare and their rescuer. Grace Dalton glanced at the headline as she folded the washing, "have a go hero, eh" she said, "don't see many of those around."

"I think we'll be going to Badminton this week," Maisie winked knowingly at Chrissie and kicked her gently under the table.

Mrs Dalton cast an eye over the giggling girls. "Are you staying for lunch Maisie," she asked, "there's a chicken in the oven."

"Yes, please, Mrs Dalton," Maisie said, unable to resist Chrissie's mum's cooking, "then you two finish folding this laundry and I'll make a start on the veg."

The girls duly obliged. "What about Kenny and Rab?" Chrissie whispered as they folded. "We'd be two-timing them if we saw Tommy and Ian Brown as well?"

"SO?" mouthed Maisie. "So, that's not very nice is it?"

Maisie shushed her with a look. "We're just......playing the field," she said, "there's no harm in that." But both Maisie and Chrissie knew, they were now playing with fire.

-----oOo------

Chapter 25

Ian Brown couldn't believe his eyes when Maisie and Chrissie came into the hall and neither could Fiona.

"I thought we'd seen the back of them," she said airily, "but I suppose like bad pennies they continue to turn up."

Ian felt his annoyance at Fiona's caustic remarks turn to anger. "They're not bad pennies," he said icily, "they're just like you and me, out to enjoy a game of Badminton."

Fiona raised her eyebrows, "stop trying to defend the indefensible, Ian," she said equally coldly, "they're just a couple of factory workers from Keiller's, Catriona McPhee told me and she's James Keiller's Secretary, so she should know," she ended emphatically.

Ian fought back his anger. "You're a SNOB, Fiona Campbell," he told her bluntly "and I don't want anything more to do with you. And," he added for good measure, "I'd appreciate if you kept your opinions about Maisie Green to yourself." With that, Ian walked calmly over to Maisie and with a smile wider than a mile, he asked her to join him on the court.

Chrissie tried to hide her smile as she strolled over to Fiona. "Fancy a game?" she said, "it looks like your usual partner is 'otherwise engaged.'"

With a withering look, Fiona returned the cover to her racket and picked up her blazer. "No thanks," she said through gritted teeth, "I've got better things to do." And

The Green Years

with a final glare towards Maisie and Ian Brown, Fiona walked out of the hall.

Once out into the cold air, she blinked furiously, as tears began to trickle from her eyes. She truly loved Ian Brown and saw a real future for them together, but not now, he'd made his choice she thought bitterly and he'd chosen a common factory worker over her.

Maisie giggled and flirted with Ian, as he tried to teach her the correct way to serve, but it was no use, Maisie was never going to be a Badminton player and Ian loved her all the more for it.

"C'mon," he said, "I think we both need a drink." As before, Ian filled the glasses with orange squash and sat alongside Maisie, he wasn't going to miss this opportunity, not like he had the last time.

"I've got some time off this week," he said, turning her head towards him, "so how about you and me going out to dinner, somewhere special," he added "to celebrate my new found fame?"

Maisie blushed. DINNER! The word reverberated through her chest. She'd never been out to dinner with a man before and because of her re-kindled affection for Kenny, wasn't quite sure how to respond. Her mind raced, Kenny was at the T.A. camp till Saturday and she wasn't his actual girlfriend or anything, so......"Why not," she said, "when were you thinking?"

"Great," said Ian, "so how about Thursday night?"

Maisie pretended to consider her availability. "Thursday should be fine," she said coyly.

"Then if you tell me where you live, I'll pick you up about six thirty and book the table for seven. Does the Angus Hotel sound alright?"

Before she had time to answer Chrissie came over, hot and red-faced. "Given up already?" she asked Maisie plonking herself down beside her friend.

"Maisie's just agreed to go out to dinner with me on Thursday," blurted out an elated Ian.

Chrissie's eyes widened.   So that was why Fiona was so upset. Maisie had won.

"Ian's picking me up at my house in his car," Maisie said briskly and before Chrissie could stop her, she told Ian **Chrissie's** address.

Ian couldn't stop grinning. "See you Thursday then," he said, taking Maisie's hand and kissing it, "can't wait."

"What's going on?" Chrissie asked after Ian had left them, "and why did you give him MY address."

Maisie was beginning to feel uneasy. Why hadn't she given Ian her own address, but she already knew the answer.

"You have a nice house," Maisie explained "and your mum and dad are nice and, well, everything about your place is nice and then there's our house....and can you imagine Ian knocking on the door and mum answering it?"

"He's not taking your mum out to dinner Maisie," Chrissie said softly, "he's taking YOU."

"I know," Maisie agree, feeling ashamed of herself, "but he's so sophisticated Chrissie and well, we aren't."

"So that's it," said Chrissie, as they made their way slowly home, "you don't think you're good enough."

Maisie nodded glumly. "I don't know what I was thinking Chrissie, once he finds out who I really am, that'll be the end of it."

Chrissie put her arm around her friend. "We're a right pair," she said, "here's me thinking you were the best thing since sliced bread and here's you thinking you're a doughnut."

Both girls burst out laughing. "It's not funny," said Maisie, "what am I going to do?"

"I thought you were doing what you wanted to do, be a two-timer." Maisie stopped in her tracks, two-timing

The Green Years

Kenny wasn't turning out to be as much fun as she'd thought it would.

"Well," she decided, shakily, "I'll go out with Ian, but just this once and Kenny must never find out. Agreed?"

Chrissie agreed, but the way Ian Brown made Maisie feel about herself wasn't good and she'd make sure she never went out with him again, whether Kenny found out or not.

The girls never spoke of the upcoming dinner date till they were leaving work on Thursday.

"So, I'll get changed and come over to your place around six," Maisie said, hurrying towards the bus, "and make sure you answer the door and not your mum or dad. They'll ask too many questions. The subterfuge was already getting to Maisie and by the time she was ready to be picked up by her date, she was feeling sick.

"I can't go through with this," she told Chrissie, but just then there was a knocking on the door.

"He's here," hissed Chrissie, "c'mon, follow me."

At the door, Chrissie pushed Maisie to the front and leaning past her, turned the handle.

The door swung open and Ian Brown stood before Maisie, a bunch of roses in one hand and his car key in the other.

"Your carriage awaits you my lady," he said, bowing slightly and offering Maisie the flowers. Maisie's heart was thudding so much she thought she was going to faint. She accepted the flowers and allowed herself to be led to Ian's car.

This was what she'd dreamed about happening to her for a long, long time, but now that it was actually happening, she felt so scared she could hardly breathe.

But the drive into town to the Angus Hotel was only the beginning. Ian parked the car and took her arm as they walked to the hotel restaurant.

"Shall I take your coat, madam?" asked the girl behind the desk at the cloakroom. Maisie shook her head.

The maitre de pointed to a table for two, candles glowed and silver cutlery was glittering in their light. Other diners were already at their tables, necklaces sparkling on the women and dinner jackets worn by some of the men. Maisie's eyes couldn't take it all in. She'd never in her life been to anywhere so posh.

She looked down at her only dress. Cheap cotton and ill fitting.

She couldn't go through with it.

"I'll just visit the lav....ladies," she said nervously, to Ian, "won't be long."

"I'll wait for you at our table," Ian said smoothly, "by the window."

Maisie turned away her heart quickening with every carpeted step. She walked past the cloakroom, the ladies toilets and the waiters bringing food to the tables, then down the stairs to the revolving door. Once through the door, she started to run and didn't stop till she was breathless.

The bus bore the reluctant princess back to Fintry and Chrissie's door.

"What happened!" Chrissie asked, her concern for her friend increasing as she rushed past her and into the bedroom.

Maisie could hold it in no longer. "It was awful," she wailed, mascara and tears blackening her cheeks "and I ran away."

Maisie held on to her till the weeping ceased and Maisie had used up half a box of tissues mopping up her tears.

"Why do I keep trying to be something I'm not?" she asked herself and Chrissie simultaneously, There was a knock on Chrissie's bedroom door and Grace Dalton popped her head around. "Everything OK," she said, knowing that everything wasn't OK. She'd heard Maisie's sobs even with the television turned up.

"I've made some hot chocolate," she said, "in the kitchen."

"That would be nice Mrs Dalton," Maisie said, "I haven't eaten all day."

The trio trooped through to the kitchen and Maisie related the whole story to Chrissie's mum. "So, I ran away," she said, "just like a silly little girl."

"Maisie, Maisie," Grace Dalton said kindly, "there's nothing wrong with wanting to better yourself and there's nothing wrong with wanting to meet new people to go out with. Where you've gone wrong is thinking that you're not good enough." She hugged Maisie and held both girls hands, "that's all."

"So, be your beautiful selves, both of you and I bet Ian Brown is sitting in the Angus Hotel right now, eating a lonely dinner and wondering where he went wrong?"

Maisie brightened. "You think so?"

"I know so," Grace said, "so finish your chocolate and get a good night's sleep, tomorrow is another day and things will look better in the morning."

"Thanks, Mrs Dalton," Maisie said, "you always know what to say to make things right."

Chrissie saw Maisie to the door. "Are you OK now?" she asked.

"I just feel a bit of an idiot," Maisie said, "and the next time I talk about two-timing being fun, remind me of tonight."

Ian Brown slowly realised that the girl of his dreams had vanished. "Could someone check the Ladies?" he asked the waiter who was hovering over the table with the wine list, "my friend wasn't feeling too well."

"Certainly sir." He returned with a shake of his head.

Ian ordered a large glass of wine, his appetite having deserted him. Something had gone wrong, but what?

He took out the slip of paper he'd written Maisie's address on.

Tomorrow he'd find out. He was too close to making her his own to give up now.

-----oOo-----

Chapter 26

The week's T.A. basic training at Barry Buddon had been gruelling. The assault course, the square-bashing and the rifle range had all been relished by Kenny, but for Rab, it was a different story. He hated everything about the T.A. and for reasons best known to himself, Shug Reilly had been on his case from day one.

"I've had enough," he told Kenny as they were marched out of the camp and back into 'civilisation.' I know you think it impresses the lassies, but if that's what it takes to get Chrissie, then I'll just have to look elsewhere for love."

"You don't mean that Rab," Kenny said, trying to placate his pal, "Shug Reilly was a bastard for sure, but he won't always be in charge, so what do you say.......think again?

But Rab wasn't to be moved on this one. "I've tried Kenny," he said, dejection sitting heavy on his broad shoulders, "but it's just not for me."

Kenny knew when to quit bugging his pal, he saw that Rab really hated all that muck and bullets, but he had loved it, regardless of whether it impressed Maisie or not.

"OK pal," he said, patting Rab on the shoulder. "Thanks for trying anyway and the next time I go to Rodd Road, I'll let them know what you've decided and find out how to return your kit."

Rab looked crestfallen. He hated letting Kenny down, but it was as well done now than later when he was in too deep.

Once they were home, Rab decided he'd go round to Chrissie's house and tell her he was no longer a soldier and if she didn't like it, then that would be that.

Ian Brown parked his car outside what he thought was Maisie's house and took a deep breath. He tucked a box of chocolates under his arm and walked resolutely up the Dalton's garden path. Grace Dalton opened the door to his knock. She was about to tell him that she didn't buy anything on the doorstep when she saw the chocolates.

"Yes?" she said, quizzically.

"I'm sorry to bother you Mrs Green, but I was wondering if Maisie was home?"

"Maisie?"

"Yes, your daughter."

"I have a daughter," Grace said, "but she's not called Maisie, nor is she called Green."

Ian looked confused. "But this is where I picked her up last night," he said, showing Grace Dalton the slip of paper.

It began to dawn on Grace who this young man might be.

"And your name is?"

"Brown," he said, "Ian Brown."

"And you picked Maisie up here last night?"

"I did."

"I think you'd better come in," Grace said, "I think there may have been a bit of a misunderstanding."

She stood aside and Ian entered the hallway.

"Over there," she said, "into the kitchen."

She put on the kettle and glanced at the unhappy young man at her table. So, this was who Maisie had run away from last night and why she came back to seek Chrissie out for comfort.

"Tea alright?" she asked. Ian Brown nodded.

Grace Dalton had some explaining to do and on Maisie's behalf.

For the next hour she told him of Maisie's upbringing and her pride in getting promoted to being a Bonus Checker at Keiller's, but most of all, for her efforts in trying to make something of her life instead of just drifting like so many others had done.

Ian listened intently. "How old are you?" Grace finally asked.

"Twenty two."

"Maisie's seventeen," Grace said, "just turned. Can you imagine how daunting it must have been for her to cope with dinner in the Angus Hotel, no matter how well intentioned you were?"

Ian grimaced. "I need to talk to her," he said determinedly, "make her understand, it's her that I........love.....not her job or her school, or anything else for that matter."

Grace Dalton smiled. She liked Ian Brown and could see why Maisie did too, but she could also see why she felt she wasn't good enough for this handsome young man.

Grace stood up and began clearing away the tea things.

"Maisie will be here on Christmas Day," she said, "she always comes for her dinner with us." She levelled her eyes with Ian Brown's. "If you're really serious about Maisie," she said, "then come back on Sunday around six o'clock. We'll be finished eating by then and those chocolates might just be appreciated."

Grace was aware that she was match-making, but she also knew instinctively that this was Maisie's best chance of making a good marriage for herself.

"Christmas Day it is," Ian said, handing Grace the box of chocolates, "and thanks for understanding." Grace looked at the proffered box. "I'll bring some more on Sunday," Ian said smiling, "you deserve them for being so kind."

Rab was just coming up the street to Chrissie's door when it opened and a man stepped out onto the path. He shook hands with Mrs Dalton and walked to his car. Rab could see a dog on the back seat that jumped up at the window when the man opened the car door, got in and drove away.

Rab froze in his tracks. The man seemed very friendly with Chrissie's mother he thought, his mind going into overdrive.

Was this the sailor who'd left Chrissie and gone back to sea? Rab had heard the rumours and felt sick. All that T.A. training nonsense and Chrissie had already got someone else. She couldn't even wait a week!

So much for impressing Chrissie in his T.A. uniform at New Year, it wasn't even Christmas and he'd been upstaged already by a bloody seaman.

He had to see Kenny. He'd know what to do.

Rab looked even more desolate when he turned up at Kenny's house. "What's up mate?" Kenny asked, "changed your mind?"

Rab shook his head, "Can I come in?" he asked, "it's about Chrissie."

"'Nuff said." Kenny stood back and watched Rab as he sidled past him and into the kitchen.

"Sorry, there's no drink," Kenny opened, "unless you want tea."

"No thanks," Rab said, sitting down. "I've just seen him."

Kenny frowned. "Seen who?"

"The sailor."

Kenny poured himself a tea and sat down opposite Rab. "What are you talking about big man?"

"I was on my way to see Chrissie, about not being in the T.A. anymore and I saw him." Rab gathered his overheated thoughts. "He was coming out o' her house and shaking hands with her mum as well! Bastard."

Kenny waited. "And he had a car Kenny," he added dismally, "how can I compete wi' a man and a car?"

Kenny digested the information.

"And how do you know he was that sailor boy Chrissie fancied?"

Rab's eyes blurred. "Well, who else could it have been?"

Kenny shrugged. "Could've been the Insurance man, a man from the council, McGills man......" Kenny was running out of options. "C'mon Rab," he said, "it could have been ANYBODY?"

"It was him," Rab stated defiantly, "he looked like a sailor."

"What, like wi' a sailor hat on or a kitbag slung over his shoulder."

But Rab wasn't to be placated. "I know Kenny, a'right," he said "I just know."

"Well, if you're right Rab," counselled his pal, "then you've two choices." Rab brightened, there were choices?

"You can either find another lassie, or you can knock his block off the next time you see him."

"Gee thanks pal," Rab said, more dejected than ever. He didn't want another lassie, he wanted Chrissie and as for knocking the sailor's block off, he'd probably set that dog on him if he tried.

Kenny tried another tack. "It's Christmas this weekend," he said, "let's hit the town and paint it red," he suggested, "and forget about all women till the New Year, then we'll see who Maisie and Chrissie fancy." He nudged Rab suggestively, "and no prizes for guessing Maisie's preference."

-----oOo------

Chapter 27

Maisie was in thoughtful mood when Chrissie called in on Christmas Eve.

"Mum asked if you're coming for Christmas Dinner, as usual?

"Of course, I am," Maisie responded, "it's the best dinner in the world."

Chrissie beamed. She did have a lovely mum, but she didn't know that she had been match-making Maisie and Ian Brown.

"What a mess I've made of things," Maisie said absently, fluffing up the blond curls round the back of her neck.

Chrissie raised her eyebrows questioningly, "you've got Kenny Wilson falling at your feet Maisie Green, so how messy do you think things are?"

"I'm not talking about Kenny," Maisie said, wistfully, "I'm talking about running away from Ian Brown, so much for being grown-up and sophisticated."

Chrissie wished she had Maisie's problem. She was torn between Rab and Tommy Murphy and no matter how hard she tried to decide who to go with, she just couldn't."

"Maybe none of them are Mr Right?" Chrissie suggested, "just like Rab and Tommy, I don't know how to choose between them either."

Maisie looked at her friend. Once again, she'd forgotten that Chrissie had boy problems too, she was so busy focussing on herself.

The Green Years

"But, I thought you'd decided on Rab?" Maisie said, "you and him seemed to be getting on really well at the pictures last week, and he does love you, you know?"

Chrissie sighed and started turning the silver bracelet around on her wrist. Maisie grabbed her arm. "When did you start wearing that again?" she asked, surprised. The last time she'd seen Chrissie, she'd put Tommy's token of love into the darkness of her dressing table drawer.

"I thought I'd wear it for Christmas," she said, too casually.

"Does this mean you're going to meet him on Hogmany?"

Chrissie shrugged. This was like pulling teeth.

"Chrissie?" Maisie said with a big question mark in her voice, "it was you who told me about two-timing being dangerous and now you're saying that's exactly what you're intending to do."

Chrissie folded her arms across her chest.

"Maybe," she said.

There was silence, while Maisie processed Chrissie's answer.

"I thought we were meeting the boys at the City Square to see the New Year in and well, see how we felt about them then, in their uniforms and all?"

Chrissie folded her arms tighter.

"And what if I fall for Tommy again when I see him" she said defensively, "and I don't want to see Rab ever again?"

Maisie was unsure of how to answer her. She'd never really forgiven Tommy for running off and hurting Chrissie like he did, but then again, hadn't she done the same thing to Ian Brown?

She leant closer to Chrissie. "Maybe neither of us should make any choices till we have to, let's just enjoy your mum's Christmas cooking on Sunday and hope, when the time comes, we choose with our hearts."

There had been a sprinkling of snow overnight and Christmas morning was one of those days when the sun shines and the sky is bright blue but it's bitterly cold.

"I've made you your favourite breakfast for Christmas," Maisie's mum said, scrambling eggs while bacon crisped under the grill along with the bread. There were no signs in the Green household that Christmas had arrived, there were no decorations nor Christmas trees with fairy lights, but that didn't matter. Maisie knew how little money there was to spare and how much had been spent on her breakfast, while her mum settled for porridge. "Keeps me regular," she always said, patting her stomach.

"Dad still in bed?" Maisie asked, spreading the hot toast.

Mrs Green nodded. "Had a bad night," she said, "hardly slept a wink for the pain in his back and legs."

Maisie grimaced. How unlucky her parents had been. Not for them the security of a decent wage and nice things, they'd been stuck with their 'hand to mouth' existence for years now with Maisie's board money often being the only thing that prevented the family from falling into debt.

The plateful of bacon and scrambled eggs was placed before her. "Thanks mum," she said, feeling a lump of emotion form in her throat. How she wished things could have been different for her mum, be more like Grace Dalton, who seemed to have everything, thanks to her husband's good job at Timex.

"Are you going to Chrissie's for your dinner as usual?" her mum asked, breaking into her thoughts.

Maisie nodded, not wishing to dwell on the differences in lifestyle. Grace Dalton will have decorated her living room with red paper bells and tinsel and a Christmas Tree twinkling with lights and coloured baubles. Maisie looked around the shabby kitchen. Although she loved her mum, the thought of living a life like hers filled her with dread.

She finished her breakfast more determined than ever that, for her, life was going to be better.

"Come away in Maisie," Grace Dalton smiled as she opened the door, "I hope you've brought your appetite?"

Maisie shrugged out of her coat and smoothed the front of her thick jumper over her skirt. "And leave your boots in the hall, Maisie," Mrs Dalton called over her shoulder. There's a pair of Chrissie's slippers there for you."

Maisie did as she was bid and with toes cosying nicely in the furry lining she went into the wonderland that Grace Dalton had created.

"Merry Christmas Maisie," grinned Mr Dalton, shaking her hand while at the same time kissing her on the cheek, "how's mum and dad?"

"Dad's in a bit of pain," Maisie said, trying not to dampen the mood, "but they're both OK."

"Good," said Chrissie's dad, as he guided her to her chair at the table, which was gleaming with polished cutlery and glasses and a gold-coloured Christmas Cracker at each place.

"Mrs Dalton's been chopping and mixing all morning," he continued, "and if the smells that are now coming from the kitchen are anything to go by, our Christmas Dinner is on its way."

The tomato soup was delicious, the roast chicken in its rich gravy melted in the mouth and by the time they'd finished eating their Christmas Dumpling and custard, everyone was full to the brim.

"Grace," announced John Dalton, "that was your best ever Christmas dinner," he said, his face flushed with the heat from the fire and the Whisky. Grace beamed. She loved making a fuss of her family and Christmas was by far the best time to indulge her generous nature.

"It's not over yet," she smiled, moving towards the Christmas tree and pulling gaily wrapped parcels from under its branches.

She handed out a present for everyone. "Merry Christmas," she piped "and a Happy New Year, when it comes."

Maisie glanced over at Chrissie. The mention of the New Year, brought both girls back to their impending meeting with the boys.

"Open your gifts then girls," Grace urged excitedly, her eyes sparkling with fun.

Chrissie revealed some new pyjamas while Maisie unwrapped a matching scarf and bobble hat.

"Perfect," both girls said, grinning at the choices Grace Dalton had made, certain that she still believed them to be children and not the sophisticated beauties they saw when they looked in the mirror.

John's gift to his wife was a Timex watch and a string of pearls and hers to him was a hip flask for his Whisky.

The hands on the clock moved to six and Grace and the girls began clearing the table while John Dalton took his place at the fireside with another glass of Whisky and his Christmas cigar.

At six o'clock on the dot, there was knocking at the front door.

"Can you get that Maisie," Grace Dalton asked, indicating her rubber gloves and soapy water.

Chrissie looked confused. "Are we expecting anyone else on Christmas day?" she asked. Grace held her gloved finger to her lips. "Ssshhhh," she said, "it's a surprise for Maisie."

Ian Brown had been sitting in his car for the past 30 minutes watching as the clock on the dashboard ticked its way to six.

The Green Years

This was his moment to convince Maisie of his intentions and he wasn't sure whether it was the cold or the fear of rejection that was making his legs shake.

Then, suddenly, she was standing there at the open door, blinking in the gloom and hardly able to believe her eyes.

"Ian?"

Ian Brown smiled. "Maisie?"

"What are you doing here?" she asked, her mind trying to understand what was happening.

"I've come to see you," he said simply, "and if you'll let me, I'd like to show you something."

Just then Grace Dalton came up behind Maisie and placed an arm around her shoulder.

"He came looking for you Maisie," she said softly, "and I told him where to find you on Christmas Day."

Maisie's eyes widened, but before she could say another word, Ian spoke. "I'll wait for you in the car," he said, "till you get your things." He took a step back from the doorway, "but if you want to run away again, I'll understand."

Mrs Dalton guided Maisie back into the hall. "He's a good man, Maisie," she said, "and I think you should hear him out."

Maisie's heart was thudding in her chest. It all seemed unreal and she felt that at any minute she would find it was a dream and waken up.

"Go," Grace urged, handing Maisie her coat, "he's waiting for you."

Chrissie, fed up of waiting for everyone to return to the kitchen came into the hall as Maisie was pulling on her boots.

"Where are you going?" she asked, "we haven't played Charades yet?"

"Maisie has to go now," Grace said, "she's got an unexpected Christmas present waiting for her outside."

Chrissie's eyebrows drew together in confusion.

"It's Ian Brown," Maisie said, her voice quiet with shock, "he wants to show me something."

The snow that had threatened earlier began to fall around Maisie as she walked down the path to Ian's car. He jumped out of the driver's seat and hurried round to the other side of the car and opened the door for her.

"Thanks Maisie," he said, "for not running."

Grace and Chrissie watched as Ian with Maisie on board, drove off.

"C'mon Chrissie," Grace said, "let's get those dishes done and there's still my Christmas Cake to eat."

Chrissie didn't know quite how it had happened, but it seemed that by some mysterious manoeuvring of her mother, Maisie's fate was about to be decided.

-----oOo-----

Chapter 28

Ian Brown drove carefully through the thickening snow out of Fintry and up the Forfar Road before turning into Clepington Road.

Not a word passed between them on the drive and it wasn't until Ian slowed the car and pulled up outside a tenement building that he spoke.

"Well, here we are," he said, indicating the building.

Maisie looked past Ian searching for some explanation of what exactly Ian wanted to show her.

"Do you trust me enough to come with me......in there?"

Maisie hesitated. This was all too unreal, like the posh dinner had been, but this time she steeled herself not to run.

She nodded, "I think so."

"Don't look so scared Maisie, "he said, "it's just where me and Rebel live."

Maisie's eyes opened in surprise. Ian Brown lived here!

She'd always imagined him living in a big house somewhere far away from Fintry, where people went to the theatre and ate in posh hotels.

"Rebel's been looking forward to wishing you Merry Christmas," he said, grinning "and so have I."

Maisie suddenly felt foolish and naive as she allowed Ian Brown to help her from the car and hold on to her as they made their way into the close and Ian Brown's flat.

Rebel heard them coming before he saw them and was whining at the door as Ian unlocked it.

"Hey boy," he said, holding the dog's paws as Rebel reared up on his hind legs, "look who's here?"

Maisie gazed at the beautiful animal as she remembered the last time they'd met and she'd shaken 'paws' with Rebel. She'd been rescued by the dog and his master from two thugs who'd followed Maisie and Chrissie in the Den o' Mains.

She bent down and stroked Rebel's head. "Merry Christmas," she said, beginning to relax, "and thanks again for rescuing us."

Ian hung her coat and Christmas hat and scarf on the hook behind the door before taking Maisie's hand and guiding her through another door into Ian's front room.

The warmth spilled out into the little lobby as the door swung open and Maisie could see a fire burning in the grate, coloured chains of paper looping across the ceiling and a little Christmas tree twinkling brightly at the window. A low table was set with two wine glasses and a bottle of red wine, along with a plate bearing mincemeat pies.

Maisie felt tears forming in her eyes. Ian Brown had done this specially for her?

"Please Maisie," he said, "we need to talk."

"This," he said, indicating his surroundings, "is ME. I've lived here for three years now, two of them when I was an engineering student and then this last year, since I've been working at the NCR.

Dad died a year ago," Ian continued, his voice dropping at the memory, "that's his car I've got, and I had to give up the engineering course to look after mum. She's a bit better now and I'm hoping I'll be able to get back to engineering next year."

The Green Years

Ian opened the wine and poured out two glasses, handing one to Maisie. "Merry Christmas," he said, "I hope."

Maisie took a tiny sip of the red liquid.

"Now it's your turn," Ian said, "tell me all about Keiller's and your mum and dad and life in wintry Fintry....." Ian smiled inwardly at the look of disbelief on Maisie's face. How did he know so much about her?

Ian removed the wine glass from Maisie's hand and replaced it with his own warm grasp. "I went looking for you after you disappeared at the Angus Hotel that night and found Grace Dalton at the address you gave me. She told me why you'd left and I knew that, somehow, I had to let you know how wrong you've been about everything and me in particular."

Maisie allowed her mind to ease, as the pieces of the jigsaw fell into place. "So," Ian said quietly, "can we start again Maisie?"

Maisie felt very still inside. She'd longed for Ian Brown to fall in love with her and now that he seemed to have, the rush of desire for him she'd expected to happen, just didn't! Somewhere deep inside there was a hesitation which she couldn't ignore. Now that Ian Brown was available to her, she wasn't sure at all if he was 'the one.'

She needed time to think. What about, she didn't know, she only knew that now wasn't the time to make her mind up about Ian Brown.

"Can I sleep on it?" she asked, her eyes giving nothing away, "it's all been a bit of a shock you see," she added, extricating her hand from his "and maybe you should meet my mum and dad before we go any further...." her voice tailed off as she ran out of excuses not to tell Ian Brown what he now desperately wanted to hear.

"Right," Ian said flatly, "if that's what you want."

Ian stood up, as did Rebel, thinking it was time for his walk.

"I'd better take you home then," he said, leaving Maisie in the room while he got her things from the lobby.

Rebel sat on the floor beside her and rested his head on Maisie's lap. "Sorry, boy," she whispered, "for ruining your master's Christmas."

The drive back to Fintry was treacherous, the snow was lying thickly now and only traffic that needed to be out was on the road. The windscreen wipers were barely sweeping the snow clear before it began to form again. Maisie clung to the door handle, bracing her feet against the floor as the car slithered around the corner of Clepington Road onto Forfar Road.

Ian's knuckles were white as he gripped the steering wheel, cursing himself for being so stupid as to drive in this weather, but continuing the evening with Maisie after her lukewarm response to his overtures had forced the issue.

Forfar Road dipped steeply towards its junction with the Kingsway where the car began to veer alarmingly into the kerb as it skidded out of control. Ian jerked the wheel and stabbed at the brakes, but only managed to speed their descent even more. It was the iron lamp post that stopped them from careering onto the Kingsway, but its impact catapulted both of them into the windscreen.

Esther Green was beginning to wonder where Maisie had gotten to, when there was a knock at her door. "She's probably forgotten her key again," she muttered, but when she opened the door two policemen towered over her. "Mrs Green," said one of them, "is your man in?"

Esther stepped backwards, "Joe," she called, alarm shaking her vocal chords, "can you come to the door..... it's the police!"

Joe Green shuffled up the lobby, peering over his reading glasses. The police never brought good news and he felt his stomach tighten.

"Whut is it?" he asked putting his hand on Esther's shoulder.

"Can we come in Mr Green?"

Joe Green nodded and stepped back allowing the bobbies to come in.

"I believe Maisie Green is your daughter?"

Esther felt faint. "Maisie," she said hoarsely, "is she alright?"

"There's been a bit of an accident Mrs Green, Maisie's been hurt quite badly and she's in DRI."

Joe and Esther Green were hit by a bolt of fear. "She's alright though," Joe said. The policeman nodded, "she's in good hands," he said, "we've got the car outside, so if you could get your coats we'll drive you to the hospital."

Joe and Esther trembled silently during the journey, each afraid to voice their worst fears.

"She's in here," the doctor said, leading the way along a corridor to a side ward. "She's a bit drowsy," he said quietly into the hush of the ward, "her arm was broken when the car hit the lamp post and she was badly concussed when they found her, so she'll be out of action for a while, but hopefully, she'll make a full recovery."

The doctor faded back into the dimness as Joe and Esther tiptoed cautiously to Maisie's bedside. "What was she doing in a car?" Esther whispered to her man. Joe didn't answer.

"Maisie," he called gently, "are you awake lassie?"

Maisie's eyes fluttered open as the sound of dad's voice filtered through the effects of the chloroform. "Dad?"

"Sssshhhhh Maisie," Joe said, "you've had a bit of an accident and you're in DRI, but everything's fine and the doctor says you'll soon be on your feet again." He turned and looked at his wife. "Mum's here too," he said, moving aside to let Esther in to the bedside. "Maisie," she whispered, "it's your mum."

Maisie felt her hand being squeezed, before she fell back into her anaesthetised sleep.

When Chrissie and her mother heard the news of the car accident, their first thoughts were for Maisie. "Is she going to be alright Esther?" Grace asked, pouring cups of tea for all of them.

"What I can't understand is what she was doing in a car and in that weather?"

Grace and Chrissie exchanged glances. Time for the truth.

"She was with a young man called Ian Brown," Grace said, "and I think he must have been driving her home or something when the accident happened."

"Ian Brown?"

"It's her boyfriend," Chrissie stated, "at least I think it is. She met him at the Badminton Club."

"Nobody ever tells me anything," Esther muttered to herself, getting back to normal now she knew Maisie was going to be fine.

"Can we see her?" Chrissie asked, "at the hospital I mean."

"Not today," said Esther, "but tomorrow I'm sure she'd like a visit." Grace nodded agreement. "She'll be more like herself then."

Esther finished her tea, taking an appreciative look around Grace Dalton's house as she left. Some women have all the luck, she thought, fervently hoping that Maisie would be one of them.

"What do you know about Ian Brown?" Grace asked anxiously after Esther had left.

"Only that he goes to the Badminton Club and he's a security guard at the NCR. He was in the paper recently, don't you remember, he caught a couple of thieves breaking into the factory grounds."

Grace pondered the news. "I'm going to telephone the DRI," Grace said decisively, "find out if he's been admitted as well."

The Admissions Office were less than helpful as Grace wasn't a relative, so they couldn't give out any personal information about their patients.

"However," said the Receptionist, "I can say that an Ian Brown was admitted on 25th December and discharged the next day."

A wave of relief washed over Grace. "Thank goodness," she said to her daughter, who'd been crushed into the phone box beside her.

"Let's wait and see how Maisie is tomorrow," Grace said, "I feel easier now I know Ian is alright." Grace Dalton had somehow felt responsible for what had happened, having engineered the fateful meeting. In future, she would keep her good intentions towards Maisie to herself.

-----oOo-----

Chapter 29

Kenny and Rab were in the doldrums. "This is so boring," said Kenny, "all the pub's are shut and this snow's gonna be lying 'till New Year at least."

At the thought of New Year, however, he brightened up.

"Can't wait till the Bells," he said, "when me and Maisie finally get to 'going steady.'" He finished off his can of Export and smiled at the thought. Rab grunted.

"Are you still mopin' about that sailor?" Kenny asked.

Rab's hair was beginning to grow, just a little and by the time the New Year came around, he'd be back in his drainpipes and drape jacket, but he'd be without Chrissie.

"Nope," he said, catching the can of beer Kenny had tossed over to him.

"Then cheer up big man," he responded cheerfully, "there's plenty more fish in the Tay."

Rab grunted again. "For you maybe," he said morosely, "with your new uniform and all."

"Look," said Kenny soothingly, "maybe you've got it all wrong and Chrissie's just longing to see you again."

"Huh!"

Kenny sighed, this was pointless. "Look," he said, "get your jacket, we're going out."

"Out.....Where?"

"Where do you think," Kenny said sharply, "to Chrissie's."

The Green Years

Protesting, but not too loudly, Rab followed his pal to Chrissie's house, just in time to see Chrissie and her mother getting into a car.

Rab slithered towards the motor. If it was that sailor again, he'd be sorry this time.

"Chrissie," he shouted, "where are you going?"

Chrissie wound down the window of her dad's car and beckoned him closer.

"We're going to the DRI," she whispered, "Maisie's been in an accident and we're going to see her. Tell Kenny."

The car had slowly moved off, crunching over the impacted snow and ice as Kenny drew level with him.

"Well," he said, "what did you say?"

Rab was stunned. He turned to Kenny, hardly moving his lips they were so cold. "Maisie's in hospital," he said, "she's been in an accident."

Kenny felt the colour drain from his face.

"Is she alright?" he asked desperation taking over his usual cool facade.

"Don't know Kenny," Rab said, "Chrissie and her mum have gone to see her."

Kenny had never felt so helpless. All the army training and square bashing hadn't prepared him for this. The love of his life lay injured, possibly dying, and he'd been drinking beer.

"C'mon," said Rab, putting an arm around Kenny's shoulder.

"Let's get you home."

Kenny allowed himself to be led back to his house, all the time, berating himself for not being there for Maisie. Some boyfriend he was turning out to be. Rab made them both hot, sweet tea and forced Kenny to drink it.

"When Chrissie comes back from the hospital," he said quietly,

Sandra Savage

" I'll find out what's happened, then maybe you can go and see her for yourself."

Kenny nodded blankly. What kind of accident had she had, how badly was she hurt, why wasn't he there to save her. The more he thought about it the more inadequate he felt.

T.A. Soldier, he thought, more like chocolate soldier for all the use he was.

The light had gone from the sky and the street lights cast an eerie glow over the pavements, now piled with frozen slush, allowing just a narrow walkway for pedestrians, when Rab finally knocked on Chrissie's door.

Kenny had fallen into a drunken sleep and was 'out of it' by the time Rab had left.

Chrissie came to the door.

"I've been expecting you," she said, "you'd better come in."

Chrissie led him into the kitchen and indicated he should sit at the table. Rab had never been in Chrissie's house before and felt awed at the gadgets ranged over the worktops, especially the electric kettle which Chrissie had switched on to make them some tea.

"Is she alright?" he asked as Chrissie poured the water into the teapot.

"She's broken her arm and had a nasty bump on the head," Chrissie said, "but the doctor says she should be able to go home in a few days, as long as she takes things easy."

Tea was poured into china cups with saucers and teaspoons.

Rab felt clumsy and drank the tea, without adding milk or sugar, in one gulp.

Silence surrounded them.

"Do you know what happened?" he asked, eventually, watching while Chrissie re-filled the tiny cup.

The Green Years

"Car accident," Chrissie stated matter-of-factly. At the mention of a car, Rab bristled. That bloody sailor again, he fumed, and what was he doing with Maisie in his bloody car anyway.

He grasped the nettle. "That'll be your sailor friend's car then?" her asked through gritted teeth.

Chrissie looked at him, "sailor-friend?" she said feigning curiosity. How did Rab know about him?

"Aye," Rab continued, in for a penny in for a pound. "I saw him a couple of days ago at your house, seemed very friendly with your mum."

Chrissie tried not to smile. Rab was jealous! She felt a rush of love for him that came from nowhere. Big Rab Skelly, tough as nails and T.A. soldier, was JEALOUS.

Chrissie quickly changed the subject, she wasn't going to tell Rab the truth, just yet. "How was the T.A. training camp?" she asked, "did you get your bonnie uniform?"

Rab felt crestfallen. So, here it was, confession time.

"No," he said, taking a deep breath, "I didn't get a bonnie uniform, in fact," he concluded, "I'll not be going back."

He gulped down his second cup of black tea.

"So," he said, standing up and replacing the cup in its saucer, "I'll not be turning up at the City Square 'dressed to kill', so to speak, there'll just be me as I am. Take it or leave it."

For what seemed like an eternity, nothing was said.

Then, Chrissie spoke. "I'll take it."

Rab stopped in his tracks. "What did you say?"

"I said, I'll take it Rab Skelly," Chrissie said and she meant it, "if you'll take me as I am as well."

All thoughts of meeting Tommy Murphy again, vanished as Chrissie at last knew for certain, Rab, with all his hard exterior and clumsy shyness, was the man for her.

"So, Rab Skelly," she said softly, "will you still meet me at the City Square to bring in the New Year......just as you are?"

Chrissie felt two strong arms surround her and Rab's lips on hers. That was answer enough.

"So, who was the guy in the car?" he asked as Chrissie walked him to the front door.

"Just a friend of mum's" she lied, unwilling to say anything more about Ian Brown. Rab seemed satisfied. "I'll tell Kenny that Maisie's OK then?" he said, kissing her again.

"She'll be home before the New Year," Chrissie assured him, "so tell him not to worry."

Rab didn't want to let Chrissie go and held her closer.

"You know that I love you," he said, gruffly, "always have."

Chrissie loosened his grip and looked him full in the face, "and I love you too, Rab Skelly," she said, "and I always have as well."

Chrissie closed the door and went to her bedroom. She slipped off the silver bracelet and along with the letter from Tommy Murphy, placed them both back into the darkness of the drawer. She wouldn't be needing them anymore.

-----oOo-----

The Green Years

Chapter 30

Ian Brown quickly discovered that Boxing Day wasn't the best of times to try to get his car fixed. The police had towed it to their compound but it would be Tuesday before anything could be done. Fortunately, Ian had fared better than his motor and had been discharged by the doctors on the strict orders that he should rest up for the next few days. But that had been impossible.

He hadn't been allowed to see Maisie before he'd left the hospital but was told her condition was stable and he should check with her parents for any more information. Check with her parents, he thought, he didn't even know where they lived!

Today, he had to hand his Insurance documents in to Bell Street nick, visit his mother, who would be frantic if he didn't arrive for the usual Boxing Day tea, get in touch with NCR about missing his next shift and walk Rebel who was getting frantic to be out.

It all seemed too much to cope with and tears of shock and loneliness welled in his eyes as he tried to make sense of the whole mess.

It was Rebel who alerted him to the noise at the front door.

Ian blew his nose and pulled himself together. "Please, not more bad news" he muttered to himself as he turned the lock.

"Fiona!" he exclaimed, not sure if he was seeing things, "what are you doing.....?"

Fiona gently moved past him into the flat, taking off her gloves and scarf as she did so.

"I've come to say I'm sorry," she said bluntly, her eyes examining the backs of her hands, "I was rude and hateful about Maisie and I don't want to lose your friendship, so I've come to ask if you can forgive me?"

Ian Brown was unable to speak. How much courage had it taken for Fiona to make the journey to see him, when he'd called her a snob the last time they'd met.

Her eyes found his and she joined him in the silence.

"What's wrong?" she whispered, finally, "you've been....crying?"

"I was in a car accident," he muttered vaguely, rubbing his face with his hands to try to bring himself back to reality.

"Car accident!" Fiona exclaimed, now realising how shaken Ian looked. "Are you alright?" she asked stupidly. Of course he was alright, he was standing in front of her. "Please, sit down," she said, "I'll make you some tea."

She looked around the little room and spotted a door through to a scullery. "Won't be long," she said, "Two sugars isn't it?"

In the sanctuary of the scullery, Fiona calmed her breathing as the kettle boiled. She had debated with herself long and hard as to whether she should come to see Ian, but now, she was glad she did. He looked terrible.

She handed him a mug of tea and took a seat opposite him.

The wine bottle and two glasses were still sitting on the coffee table. One of the glasses had to have been for Maisie, Fiona surmised, but she didn't want to think about that now, she'd worry about it later.

The Green Years

Ian felt some warmth return to his heart as he drank the sweet tea. "Better?" Fiona asked.

"A bit," Ian replied, "conscious now of how it all must look.

"Is there anything I can do?" Fiona asked, quietly, "the car's at the door if you want to go to the hospital......or anything."

She knows, Ian realised, but she's still here and offering help.

Ian felt a stab of guilt. How could he have treated her so badly.

"I can't take up any more of your time," he said, "you must have other things to do on Boxing Day but........if you could....?"

Fiona took control. She looked at Rebel, whose eyes were pleading to go for a walk.

"Tell you what," she said, donning her scarf and gloves again, "I'll take Rebel out for a while, he looks like he's desperate and when I come back, if there's anything else needs doing, I'd only be too glad......"

Ian held up a silencing finger to his lips. "Rebel would really appreciate a walk," he said, looking at his dog as its ears pricked up at the mention of its name and the word 'walk.'

In the quietness that followed Fiona and Rebel's departure, Ian tidied away the glasses and wine bottle along with the mugs and changed his clothes into something warm and comfortable.

The police could wait till Tuesday to check his documents, he decided and if Fiona could give him a lift to his mother's then everything else could wait. He felt his self-control returning.

He watched from the window as Rebel pulled Fiona through the snowy pavement back home. How could he have been so cutting to her and how could he have been so wrong when he called her a snob.

Girl and dog came through the door in a flurry of snowflakes and cold air.

"It's freezing out there," Fiona said, her face flushed with the sudden heat in the flat. She unchained Rebel who immediately ran to his drinking bowl.

"You look better," she said, smiling at the difference in Ian's demeanour.

"I feel better," he said, "thanks to you."

Fiona beamed with pleasure. "ME," she squeaked, "I've just walked Rebel that's all. No need for thanks."

Ian found himself smiling back at the girl in front of him.

"I'm going to mum's for her Boxing Day tea later..." he began, but before he could ask her for a lift, Fiona offered.

"Let me drop you off," she said, quickly, "I don't think there are any buses running and with your own car out of action, it's the least I can do."

Ian felt a surge of gratitude. "Would you?" he asked, amazed at her generosity.

"Sure," Fiona said, "but only if you forgive me first."

Ian shook his head in disbelief. "Me....forgive YOU?"

Fiona waited. "Well?"

"You're forgiven," Ian said, officially, "and can you also forgive me for calling you a ...."

It was Fiona's turn to silence him. "Forgiven," she said, "and can we be friends again?"

Ian had an almost overwhelming urge to hug her.

"Friends," he said, unfastening Rebel's lead.

Tomorrow, he would go to the hospital and find Maisie and prove to her he loved her, but for today, enough was enough.

The drive to Ian's mother's house at Invergowrie was slow and cautious, but Fiona was a good driver and finally stopped safely outside the small bungalow.

Ian was conscious of the long drive she would have back to Broughty Ferry with the daylight fading fast.

"Will you be alright," he asked, "it's a bit of a drive back for you?"

Fiona smiled at him. "I'll be fine ," she said, "especially now that we're friends again."

Once again, Ian had the urge to hug her. He'd never really let himself get to know her before now and found himself wondering why?

"Friends again," he said, leaning over and kissing her on the cheek "and thanks again," he added warmly, "for everything."

He stood watching the red tail lights disappear from view before walking up the path to his mother's door.

"Ian," his mother smiled, "I was wondering if you'd manage to come to see me," she said, "what with the weather and everything...." She leaned past him as he went through the door into the warmth of his childhood home. "Where's your car?" she asked, concern in her voice as she looked up and down the street.

"At home," Ian lied, "I got a lift, so you've got me for the night."

"A lift?"

"Yes," Ian said, "a friend of mine was coming this way, so dropped me off." He took of his coat and hung it on the hallstand. "Friend?" his mother quizzed, "anyone I know?"

Ian hugged his mother. "Happy Boxing Day mum," he said, "and her name's Fiona Campbell."

Mrs Brown smiled to herself. "Fiona Campbell," she repeated, "nice name."

Rab relayed the news about Maisie, back to Kenny. "So, she's fine," he said, "should be out of hospital in a couple of days and Chrissie says you'll be able to see her then."

Kenny paced up and down the kitchen. "A couple of days!" he exclaimed, "I can't wait that long. I need to see her NOW."

"Well you can't" said Rab patiently, "it's Boxing Day and there's no buses running and you've missed the visiting hour anyway."

Kenny dropped into a chair, his legs stretched out and his hands linked over his cropped hair.

"She needs me Rab," he said tightly, "and I need to see her, see she's alright."

"Tomorrow," Rab assured him, "we'll go and see her then."

"WE," said Kenny, "who's WE?"

"You, me and Chrissie," Rab said, forgetting Kenny hadn't been told yet about Chrissie and him 'going steady.'

"Sorry Rab," Kenny said, "but this is something I need to do alone." He unlinked his fingers and leant forward in the chair.

"There's things I need to talk to Maisie about, personal things," he added, "and I can't do that if you and Chrissie are ear-wigging."

Rab felt wounded. "We wouldn't be ear-wigging Kenny," he said, hurt in his voice, "it's just that we need to tell Maisie something too."

"There's that 'WE' again, Rab, Kenny snapped, "WE WHO?"

Rab's lips tightened. He tried to understand that Kenny was upset but it still hurt when his friend spoke angrily to him.

"ME AND CHRISSIE," Rab shouted back, "that's the WE I'm talking about. And WE want to tell Maisie and you, if you'd listen, that we're going steady, OFFICIALLY."

"Whut?"

"You heard Kenny Wilson," Rab said, scowling at him and crossing his arms defensively.

"Well, I'll be blowed," Kenny whistled, leaning back again in his chair, "officially like..... getting engaged like?" he asked

Rab nodded. "I'm going to propose to her at Hogmany."

For once Kenny was lost for worlds.

"But what about the T.A. thing," Kenny said, "isn't she expecting you to turn up in your uniform"?

"Nope."

"You've told her you're not joining and she's still wanting to be your lass?"

Rab grinned to himself. "Yep."

Kenny was impressed. It looked like Chrissie loved the big man, in or out of uniform and his respect for Rab increased.

Rab was a lucky man, but how would Kenny fare when he came face to face with Maisie. Would she too, accept him in or out of uniform? Just as he was?

Tomorrow he would find out.

-----oOo------

Chapter 31

A thaw had happened overnight, and the pavements were now wet with slush but the buses were running again.

"Busy day," Mrs Brown asked over breakfast. Ian had slept in his old room last night and it was good to have him back home again, even if it was only for one night.

"One or two things I need to do," he said, without mentioning anything specific, "so I'll clear off after breakfast."

Rebel was there to greet him and rushed to the door when Ian came in.

"I know, boy," he said, clipping on his lead, "walkies." Usually, Ian would drive to Caird Park but today, it was a quick march to the Swannie Ponds and back again.

While Rebel ate his dogfood Ian washed and shaved and put on his only suit. He was going to see Maisie that afternoon and had to look his best, so after arranging with a garage to take on the repair of his car and handing in his documents at Bell Street, Ian set off for the DRI and Maisie.

On the way there, he found a florist open where he bought a bunch of Freesias and a tray of fruit, unsold before Christmas and still wrapped in cellophane topped with a red ribbon.

Afternoon visiting time was three to four o'clock and on the dot of three, Ian entered the ward, his eyes anxiously scanning the beds for Maisie.

The Green Years

She was reading a magazine and didn't see him approach and the sound of his voice made her jump.

"Ian!" she exclaimed, "you're alright......I was worried about you, but there was no one to ask....." Her voice tailed off as he handed her the flowers and the fruit basket.

"They're for you," he said, sitting down on the chair by Maisie's bed and trying to gauge her reaction to the gifts. She sniffed the Freesias and gazed at the fruit. "Thank you," she said, "but I'm not ill really..... just this....." She held up the plastered arm secured by a sling tied around her neck.

Ian grimaced, this small talk wasn't what he wanted to hear.

"I know you're not ill," he said, "but I wanted you to have them anyway....." he said, searching for the right words to say and failing. "I don't want you thinking I've been neglecting you," he rambled, "but I had to get the car fixed and visit my mother and there's Rebel, of course, he needed looking after......."

SHUT UP, he told himself, tell her that you love her, make it alright.

Maisie felt uneasy, she wasn't used to men who were so controlled and polite and didn't know quite how to react to Ian's detailed list of reasons for his delayed appearance.

"It's alright," she said, "you don't have to explain yourself to me." The silence that following lasted far too long, Ian was floundering.

"Will you be getting home soon?" he asked bleakly, beginning to realise that all the things he'd wanted to do and say had come to nothing.

"Tomorrow, I think," she said, "the doctors will be speaking to mum and dad today, but I think tomorrow........I'll be home..." again the conversation dried up.

Almost simultaneously, both Maisie and Ian realised that he still didn't even know where she lived, but neither of them broached the subject.

What was it? Maisie wondered, as Ian continued to gaze at nothing in particular. Where was the 'Have a Go Hero' she'd felt drawn to, when she'd read about Rebel and him capturing the two robbers at the NCR? The distance between them widened in the silence and despite wanting to feel some closeness, right now, all she felt was sorry for him.

Loud voices at the ward door drew Maisie's attention. She felt herself cringe as her dad, followed by her mum, came unsteadily up the ward waving at her and bristling with temper.

"They said you were only allowed two visitors at a time," her dad said, eyeing Ian Brown, "so they weren't going to let us in." Joe Green turned his full attention on Ian Brown.

"Who's this then?" he asked Maisie.

Ian stood up and offered the seat to Maisie's mother.

"This is Ian," Maisie said hastily, "the driver of the car."

Ian was unhappy about being referred to as 'the driver' and not 'my boyfriend,' but he said nothing. Instead he watched as Maisie's mother cast a puzzled eye over him, before sitting down in the chair and giving him no more heed.

Maisie's dad looked at the ward clock and then at Ian Brown.

It was obvious he'd outstayed his welcome, not just by Mr and Mrs Green, but by Maisie as well.

"I'll be in touch," he said, inanely, "and get well soon."

No one did anything to stop him, so with ears burning, he left the ward and Maisie behind.

"Who was that?" Esther Green asked her daughter, "and dressed up like a dog's dinner an'all."

"And whut possessed you to go in a car with the Wally?" added her father, dismissively.

There it was. Her mum and dad had spotted it right away. The problem wasn't that she wasn't good enough for Ian Brown, it was that Ian Brown wasn't man enough for her. The feelings of panic she had experienced at the Angus Hotel when she'd ran away and again at Ian's flat, when all she'd wanted to do was go home, had confused her, but seeing him now made her realise that what she was being offered was only the appearances of love, perfect on the surface with its wine and flowers, but what was missing was the spark of love, from his heart.

The rest of the visit blurred into words and gestures, but Maisie heard none of it. Maybe it was still the shock of the accident, maybe the thought of another year coming to an end, but whatever it was, Maisie felt empty and lost. All her plans for a better life for herself had evaporated with the departure of Ian Brown from the Ward and from her life.

The bell sounding the end of the visiting hour rang into Maisie's thoughts. "So, we'll come and get you tomorrow then," she heard her mother say, "at eleven o'clock."

Maisie forced a smile. "Great," she said, "can't wait to get home."

But get home to what? Maybe she should just stop trying so hard to change her life, maybe she needed to be more like Chrissie and let life happen to her.

The nurse came over to check her temperature. "Going home soon?" she asked. Maisie nodded, the thermometer bobbing up and down in her mouth. The nurse noted the reading on Maisie's chart. "You'll be home for Hogmany then," she said. Again Maisie nodded. "Lucky you," came the reply, "I'll be working here while all my pals will be celebrating."

Maisie could think of nothing better than missing Hogmany altogether. It was going to be miserable and maybe she could convince Chrissie to give it a miss.

The nurse gave Maisie a quizzical look. "You look a bit down in the mouth," she said, "is everything alright?"

Maisie sighed. "I feel like I've lost ten bob and found a penny," she said, "and before you ask, his name's Ian."

"Man trouble, eh! Tell me about it!"

And Maisie did just that. It all came tumbling out, while the nurse listened patiently. "So, by trying to be so clever and wanting everything my way," Maisie shrugged, "I've lost the lot."

The nurse looked at her fob-watch. "Almost time for your tea," she said, giving Maisie a kind smile. "There's plenty more fish in the sea," she assured her, "and a bonnie lassie like you isn't going to have to cast your net very far."

In spite of everything, Maisie enjoyed her mince and tatties. The nurse was right, there were plenty more blokes around and a girl should be choosy, after all, the wrong man could spell disaster. She only had to look at her own mum and dad to know that.

-----oOo-----

Chapter 32

Kenny, Rab and Chrissie moved closer to the Ward door.

"It's right quiet in there," Kenny whispered, "are you sure it's OK to go in?"

Chrissie glanced at the wall clock. "It's just gone seven," she whispered back, "not many visitors come in the evening."

Rab craned his neck. "That's her over there," he said, pointing to the blonde head asleep in the pillow.

"We'll go in first," Chrissie said, "let her know you're here."

Kenny nodded, straightening the jacket of his khaki uniform.

Holding hands Rab and Chrissie tiptoed into the quiet ward up to Maisie's bed.

"Maisie," Chrissie hissed, "are you awake?"

Maisie's eyes flickered open to the sight of her best friend and Rab Skelly leaning over her.

"I am now," she said, the beginnings of a smile crossing her face.

"How are you Maisie," Rab asked, "me and Chrissie have been worried about you."

Me and Chrissie, Maisie repeated to herself. "Are you two here together then?" she asked.

Chrissie looked shyly at her man. "That's what we've come to tell you Maisie," she said, "Rab and me.......you tell her Rab...."

"What Chrissie is trying to say is, that we're officially 'going steady'."

Chrissie used her good arm to push herself upright.

"Well," she said, a shade of doubt showing in her voice. "That's great Chrissie and you too Rab." Even as she spoke, Maisie's eyes were searching Chrissie's for confirmation that it was all true. What had happened to Tommy Murphy in the short time she'd been in hospital? The last time they'd spoken, Chrissie was determined to go to the dock gate on Hogmany morning and see how she felt about her errant sailor.

"And there's somebody else wanting to see you," Chrissie beamed, "he's waiting for us to go, so he can speak to you.....personally." The emphasis on the word 'personally' hit the mark and Maisie strained her neck towards the ward door.

"See you later, Maisie," Chrissie said, "once you're back home."

Once again, Rab took Chrissie's hand and grinning broadly, led her out of the Ward.

Maisie closed her eyes and counted to ten. When she opened them, Kenny Wilson, in full battle-dress stood before her.

Maisie was lost for words, but the look on her face was enough for Kenny to sit down and take her hand in his.

A warmth began to form in Maisie's body as Kenny's grip tightened. "Are you pleased to see me?" he asked, "I mean, really pleased?"

Maisie couldn't deny it, she was very pleased to see Kenny and he'd worn his uniform too, specially for her he'd said.

The Green Years

She felt herself blushing under his gaze. "I would have come sooner," he said, but I didn't know till yesterday what had happened. A car accident, Chrissie said?" He left the question hanging there.

"I'm fine now," Maisie said quickly, trying to change the subject of her two-timing adventure and I get home tomorrow, so all's well that ends well........." she watched in horror as Kenny picked up the card that Ian had left along with the fruit and the flowers.

"Get well soon, Maisie," he read, "hopefully, all is forgiven.

Ian x"

Maisie felt the colour drain from her face.

"Who's Ian?"

Maisie had never seen Kenny so angry. "No one" Maisie mumbled, "just a friend, that's all."

"He's obviously friendly enough to come and visit you in hospital."

Maisie clenched her teeth and fixed her eyes on the chart at the end of her bed.

"Are you going to tell me Maisie," Kenny said, his voice low and controlled. "I thought you and me had an understanding."

"There's nothing to tell," Maisie said, panic bringing an edge to her voice. "He just gave me a lift that's all and with the weather and everything, the car skidded and......"

"He gave you a lift.....where to?" Kenny cut in.

Maisie felt sick. Her lies had caught her out. She'd been so clever thinking she could play one off against the other, but now her cover was blown and Kenny was never going to speak to her again.

"He gave you a lift...WHERE TO?" Kenny asked again.

Maisie eyes began to blur. "To his flat, on Christmas Day," Maisie admitted, "he said he had something he wanted to show me."

Kenny felt a surge of anger reach down to his finger tips and he clenched his fists.

"And what did he show you?"

"NOTHING," Maisie shouted, bringing the nurse's attention to her patient.

"Where does he live?" Kenny asked through gritted teeth.

"Clepington Road," Maisie told him, now devoid of any emotion.

"Where in Clepington Road"" Kenny said.

"I don't know the number," Maisie said, "it's a tenement near the top of Mains Loan."

Kenny stood up just as the nurse came to Maisie's bed.

"What are you going to do?" asked Maisie, "really scared now at what could happen when the two men came face to face.

"What any man would do," he said in a low voice, "for the love of his woman," he added under his breath, as he stood up.

Without another word Kenny Wilson marched out of the hospital ward.

Maisie burst into tears. "Stop him," she pleaded to the nurse, "he's got it all wrong."

The nurse held Maisie's trembling hand.

"Whatever it is that's got him all riled up," she said, "I don't think a two ton truck would stop him."

The loud banging on Ian Brown's door sounded urgent and Rebel began to growl deep in his throat.

"It's alright boy," he said quietly to the dog, stroking his head before opening the door.

The tall figure of a soldier confronted him.

"Your name Brown!" he spat rather than asked.

Ian nodded, "it is," he replied, warily, feeling a sensation of danger forming in his stomach, at the sight of the angry face before him.

The Green Years

"Then step outside, "he ordered, "I've got a message for you from Maisie."

At the mention of Maisie's name, it all at once became clear to Ian. This was the boyfriend she'd gone to meet from the Badminton Club that night. The soldier.

The growl from Rebel increased as he sensed his master was in danger. "And you can shut that mutt up for a start," Kenny said, eyeing the animal for any sudden movement.

"I know why you're here," Ian said, a calm sense of defeat settling in his heart, "and it's not what you think."

"I'll be the judge of what I think," Kenny retorted, "so like I said, step out here like a man, if you can call yourself that."

The gauntlet had been thrown down but Ian Brown knew when to back off and didn't pick it up.

"If you'll just listen," he began, his mind taking control, "I'll explain everything."

Kenny stood his ground, "well," he said impatiently, never breaking eye contact with his rival, "I'm listening, and it had better be good."

Ian told of his first encounter with Maisie and Chrissie in the Den o' Mains and how he'd tried to get to know her ever since.

"But she didn't want to know me," he concluded glumly and it was Chrissie's mother that arranged for me to come to their house on Christmas Day. The Last Chance Saloon, so to speak, but again, no matter what I did to try to win her over, Maisie just didn't want to know. So when she insisted I drive her back to Fintry in the snow, I couldn't refuse and that's when I crashed the car."

Kenny felt his muscles ease. Ian Brown was no more a threat to him than a feather in the wind. What had Maisie been thinking off, he wondered, even giving this man a second thought when she had him?

Kenny straightened his army jacket and made to go.

"But just incase you're making this up," he added, "I'll check with Mrs Dalton and, if she doesn't back your story up, then………I don't have to tell you what'll happen to you."

"She'll back it up," Ian said, and although it was with total defeat now staring him in the face that he closed the door, it was also with relief that Kenny had won.

In trying to understand what had gone wrong, his thoughts went back to the hospital ward, when Maisie's parents had looked at him with disinterest knowing they had nothing in common with him, nor he with them. No wonder Maisie had rejected him, he had made her feel unsure of herself with his patronising attention and for the first time he realised that maybe it wasn't Fiona who was the snob after all, perhaps it was him.

-----oOo-----

Chapter 33

Maisie's mum and dad picked her up from the DRI to take her home. It was the day before Hogmany and, although the snow hadn't returned, the wind was from the North and icy.

"Here," he mother said, wrapping Maisie's Christmas scarf round her neck, "it's a wee walk to the bus, but your dad and me were a bit short for a taxi, with you being on sick pay this week."

"It's OK, mum," Maisie assured he, "it's just a broken bone that'll mend in a few weeks and I'll still manage my job after the New Year.... look." She raised her right arm to prove it.

Maisie was desperate to see Chrissie. She would know how Kenny was and what had happened when he'd got hold of Ian Brown. As soon as she got home and had some hot soup, she'd go round to her house and get some answers.

All the old loving feelings she'd had for Kenny had surfaced when he'd came to see her at the hospital, wearing his T.A. uniform, just for her. She'd loved him from the moment she'd met him at Keiller's and it was only her silly ideas of trying to be like Fiona Campbell that had tempted her with Ian Brown. But now, where did she stand? She didn't want to be with Ian, she knew that for sure, but with Kenny now hating her, she felt as if she was well and truly back to square one. Unloved and unlovable.

Chrissie welcomed her with open arms. "Maisie," she cried, "come in, come in."

The girls tiptoed through to Chrissie's bedroom, while her mum and dad were engrossed in a TV game show.

Maisie told Chrissie the whole sorry saga, forgetting as usual about her friend's dilemma. "So, I don't know what's happened to him and whether I'll ever see him again......oh Chrissie," Maisie blubbed, "it's over!"

"C'mon," Chrissie urged, "let's go into the kitchen and get some hot chocolate." Maisie meekly followed. "I'm seeing Rab later on," Chrissie said, "he'll tell Kenny how upset you are and find out what happened."

"Oh, I'm sorry Chrissie, I forgot you and Rab were an item now and here's me thinking of myself again."

Chrissie handed Maisie the mug of cocoa. "You could do me a favour actually, if you'd like to that is....but with all that's going on I'll understand if you say no."

"Anything," said Maisie, glad of the distraction from her own troubles. "Well," Chrissie began, "I need to meet Tommy Murphy tomorrow at the Dock Gates to give him back this."

She produced the silver bracelet from the drawer.

"I know it sounds daft, but I did love him once and he doesn't deserve to be stood up just because I've changed my mind about things." Maisie nodded, Chrissie was wise beyond her years and always considered others feelings, not like Maisie who had thought of nothing but herself and her own needs for months now. And, look where that had got her.

"So, what do you want me to do?" Maisie asked, unsure of her role in all of this.

"I want you to come with me, please. I'm not brave like you and I don't think I can do it alone."

ME BRAVE thought Maisie! She'd never felt so scared in her life and so in need of Kenny's strong arms.

The Green Years

"I'll come for you tomorrow around ten o'clock," Chrissie whispered as the girls crept to the front door, "and by then, I'll know how Kenny is and where you stand with him." She took a deep breath, "and I just hope Tommy forgives me for leading him on."

"I'm glad you've decided that Rab's the man for you," whispered Maisie, tearfully, "I just wish I'd realised Kenny was truly the only man for me."

The girls hugged. "See you tomorrow," Chrissie said softly, "and Maisie, don't worry, everything will be alright."

It was almost 9 o'clock that same night, when there was another knock at the Dalton's door. "I'll get it," said Grace Dalton, "the news will be on in a minute and I know you won't want to miss it."

The tall figure of a soldier met her eyes. "Yes?" she asked.

Kenny saluted her. "I'm Kenny Wilson," he said briskly and I need to speak to you."

Grace Dalton wasn't sure if she wanted to speak to the young man, however, when he said that he was a friend of Chrissie and Maisie, she decided to let him come in.

Like Rab, this was the first time Kenny had been in Chrissie's house and he too, couldn't help but notice how neat and well-kept everything was.

He followed Grace Dalton into the kitchen and waited 'till she'd put the kettle on and indicated for him to sit down.

Kenny clenched his hands around his folded T.A. cap.

"It's about a man called Ian Brown," he began, "he says he knows you."

Grace Dalton eyed Kenny questioningly. "He may do," she said, trying to fit together the pieces of the jigsaw that was Maisie and Christmas Day.

"I'll get right to the point," Kenny continued, "Maisie's my girl you see and this Ian Brown has been chasing after her while I was at the T.A. camp."

"Your girl?" queried Grace, in surprise. "I'm sorry, but I didn't know Maisie had a boyfriend."

"Well, she does," Kenny said determination in his voice, "and that's me."

The electric kettle clicked off and Grace crossed to the worktop to make the tea, glad of the distraction. Maisie had never mentioned a boyfriend to her, or she would never have agreed to Ian Brown calling for her on Christmas Day. She thought she was doing Maisie a favour and was quite hurt to find that she had another man all along. Maisie was a 'two-timer' Grace realised and in her efforts to see Maisie better herself, she had been responsible for the mess that was unfolding before her.

She poured the tea and sipped it thoughtfully. Ian Brown would have given Maisie a better life, she could see that as clearly as she saw her own life, but now that this soldier was sitting in front of her, she wondered if she had been wrong to push Maisie towards Ian.

"I'm sorry, Kenny," she said, "If I'd known you were Maisie's boyfriend, I wouldn't have.......interfered."

It was time for Grace to lay her cards on the table.

"Maisie's been trying to build a better life for herself for a while now," she began, "and she was managing quite well, but when Ian Brown came on the scene, it was me who saw a chance for her to really find a better way to live, like I've done with my marriage to Mr Dalton." Grace indicated the pristine kitchen bristling with chrome and red Formica surfaces. "But it was all too much for Maisie and now that I've met you, I can see that arranging for Ian to come here on Christmas Day to try to persuade her to fall for him, was wrong of me. So, don't blame Maisie for what happened, it was me who tried to be a 'match-maker' and......"

Kenny held his hand up. "Thanks for being honest Mrs Dalton," he said, returning his cap to his head. "You've cleared a few things up for me, so I won't be troubling you again."

"It's no trouble," Grace said, appreciating his straightforward manner. No wonder Maisie loved him, she thought, he may not have had the privileges that Ian Brown had, but he was his own man and proud of it.

-----oOo-----

Chapter 34

At ten o'clock on Hogmany morning, Maisie and Chrissie set off to meet Tommy Murphy. It was plain that Chrissie was anxious about the meeting and Maisie didn't want to upset her friend any further by asking about Kenny. It would have to wait till all this was over.

"Do you want me to come with you?" Maisie asked as the girls stood at the corner of Trades Lane and Dock Street.

Chrissie was tight lipped and just shook her head. Maisie had never seen her so nervous and wondered if she was regretting her decision to settle for Rab.

"There he is," Chrissie whispered, clutching Maisie's arm. "I won't be long," she added, stepping off the pavement and making a beeline for Tommy.

Chrissie's heart was thudding in her chest. Seeing Tommy again would confirm her decision to be with Rab, but what if all the desire she'd once felt for Tommy returned.

As he drew nearer, Chrissie felt a stab of confusion. He looked different, very different.

"Chrissie," he called out running towards her, "you've come!"

He threw his arms around her and went to kiss her, but she pulled back.

"What's happened to you?" Chrissie asked gazing at his head.

The Green Years

"Oh, this" Tommy said, running his fingers through his spiky blonde hair. "Me and the lads had a few things done when we docked in Thailand. "Don't you like it?"

"And what's this?" Chrissie asked, pointing to a gold ear ring looped through his left ear. Tommy fingered the ring, "it means I'm available," he said winking, "and there's this," he grinned, lifting his navy jumper to reveal the tattoo of an eagle on his chest.

If Chrissie had any doubts about choosing Rab Skelly, the sight of Tommy Murphy done up like a dog's dinner put paid to them.

"I only came to give you this," Chrissie said coolly, handing Tommy the silver bracelet "and to say we won't be meeting again......ever."

Tommy took the bracelet and slipped it into his pocket. After he had written to Chrissie asking her to meet him, his ship had docked at a port in Thailand. He'd learned a lot in that country, but most of all, he had experienced the joy of unbridled sex with a beautiful Thai girl and nothing was going to stop him going back to her, not even Chrissie. He could tell by the look on her face that his plan to reinvent himself had worked.

Chrissie was stunned at the change in the man she remembered and couldn't wait to get back to Rab and her future.

She turned to go. "Chrissie," Tommy said, his voice sounding more like the Tommy she remembered. "Be happy," he said, "and think of me sometimes."

Chrissie didn't answer, she wouldn't be thinking about Tommy Murphy ever again.

Maisie was shivering with the cold when Chrissie crossed the road back to her.

"Well," she asked, linking her arm into Chrissie's "did he take it OK?"

Chrissie looked over her shoulder at the departing Tommy.

"I think we both took it OK," she said, "let's get some hot tea and get ready for tonight."

Wallace's was packed and the hot pies and bridies were flying off the shelves. Maisie and Chrissie pushed their way through to the tearoom at the back of the shop and ordered pie and beans and a large pot of tea.

Maisie was getting more and more anxious at Chrissie's lack of information about Kenny and once the waitress had deposited their meals, she could hold back no longer.

"Well," she asked, "what did Rab have to say.....about Kenny I mean?"

Chrissie shook her head as she piled beans onto her fork.

"Hasn't seen him," she said, shrugging her shoulders. "Says he went to Kenny's house yesterday but his mum said he'd gone out early and didn't know when he'd be back." Maisie pondered the information, or lack of it. Her mind was racing. The last time she'd seen him was at the hospital and his departure to find Ian Brown had left her scared and tearful.

"So, where is he?" Maisie's voice sounded strained. Chrissie squeezed her hand, "I'm sure he's OK," she said, "he's a big boy Maisie and well able to look after himself."

This didn't help. "How do you know that?" Maisie whispered, fighting back the tears as she gazed at the plate of uneaten food. "What if Ian Brown has.......set Rebel on Kenny and killed him!"

Heads turned in their direction, as their fellow diners heard the word 'killed' and wanted to hear the rest of the conversation.

"Sssshhhh?" Chrissie whispered, "nobody's killed him!" She smiled around at the earwiggers and indicated that it was all a mistake and they should go back to their pies.

The Green Years

Maisie felt a wave of guilt hit her. This was all her fault, trying to be something she wasn't and playing one off against the other. Well, she didn't feel very clever now and if anything had happened to Kenny, she would never forgive herself.

"Listen," Chrissie whispered, handing Maisie a hankie, "I'm meeting Rab at eleven o'clock at Samuel's corner to see the New Year in, so let's both go tonight and find out what's happened. Rab's bound to know something by then."

Maisie nodded dumbly, her tears dripping onto the plaster that still encased her arm.

Slowly, Maisie forced herself to eat some of the meal and drink her tea, while Chrissie waited. "Rab says he's got something for me," she confided, trying to engage Maisie's attention in something other than Kenny Wilson.

"Says it's important," she added, now glad that she'd put the ghost of Tommy Murphy to rest once and for all and could now enjoy Rab's undivided attention.

Maisie's eyes were bleak as she listened to Chrissie's news. Almost without trying, her friend had managed to find 'the one' and she could see only happiness ahead for Chrissie and Rab. She could see none ahead for herself.

1962 was turning out to be the worst year ever.

After his visit to Grace Dalton, Kenny walked the deserted streets of Fintry, thinking about what had happened with Maisie and her dalliance with Ian Brown.

He was sure now that nothing serious had gone on between them, but Mrs Dalton's words had left their mark.

She'd encouraged the match, so that Maisie would have the chance of a better life and Ian Brown could have given her that.

By the time Kenny had reached home, he'd made up his mind.

Tomorrow, he would speak to Shug Reilly, man to man.

The girls parted company late in the afternoon. Darkness had already closed in and Maisie's arm was feeling itchy under the plaster. She wanted nothing more than to pull the bedcovers over her head and sleep through the celebrations, but she knew Chrissie would be knocking on her door at ten o'clock to insist they see the New Year in together.

As usual, Maisie's mum and dad would be their next-door neighbour's First Foot and the party would go on until the early hours. Even her parents would be having a good time.

Shimmering images of Kenny flickered through her mind, his dark looks that had so entranced her when she'd first encountered him at Keiller's, his confidence in himself and in everything he did, his smile when she'd agreed to meet him at the dancing, but most of all, Kenny in his uniform when he'd came to the hospital to see her.....and then, nothing.

It was Chrissie's knocking at her bedroom door that awoke her.

"It's ten o'clock Maisie," Chrissie said "and you're not even ready."

Maisie struggled into a sitting position and swung her legs over the side of her bed. "Sorry," she murmured absently, "I must have fallen asleep."

"Look at you," squealed Chrissie, "we're meeting Rab at eleven o'clock and if you don't get a move on, we'll be late."

"I can't go," Maisie said almost to herself, but Chrissie heard her. "I'll pretend I didn't hear that Maisie Green" she said briskly, "you can't stay in bed...IT'S HOGMANY!"

She had to get Maisie to the City Square, if she had to carry her there. Rab had insisted Maisie shouldn't be left alone at Hogmany, not with what had happened with Kenny and Chrissie had agreed with him.

The Green Years

With much cajoling and encouragement, Chrissie finally managed to get Maisie out of the house and onto the bus into town.

"Now," she said gently, "that wasn't too bad was it?"

Maisie was looking utterly miserable. Chrissie linked her good arm into her own and shut up. There was nothing she could say that was going to make the journey any easier and as soon as they met up with Rab, she'd tell him any thoughts of First Footing would be off the agenda.

Rab saw the girls weaving through the crowd towards him.

He fingered the small box in his pocket with a tremor of anxiety.

What if he'd got it wrong and Chrissie hadn't loved him as much as she'd said and she'd take one look at the ring and RUN.

"Well, here we are," Chrissie said brightly, indicating to Rab with a warning tilt of her head that Maisie was here too and not in a good state.

Not knowing what to do, Rab shook Maisie's hand. "Nice to see you Maisie," he said glancing at Chrissie for guidance. "And I'm sorry about.......Kenny and well, everything."

At that moment he could have wrung Kenny Wilson's neck.

How could he have hurt Maisie so much and then just disappear without telling anyone where he was going, even his best mate.

Asking Chrissie to get engaged was now going to be very awkward, if not impossible. Kenny had managed to ruin everyone's Hogmany.

The crowd around them was gathering momentum. Revellers waving tartan scarves and draped in tinsel surrounded them as Samuels clock ticked on. But Maisie was oblivious to it all.

Rab put his arm around her shoulder. "Cheer up, Maisie," he said, desperately, "me and Chrissie are here and........"

But before Rab could say anymore, there was a tap on his shoulder. "And don't forget me, Maisie" Kenny Wilson said to the stunned trio.

Maisie couldn't believe her eyes. Once again, Kenny Wilson in full battle-dress stood before her.

"You didn't think I'd miss Hogmany did you?" he asked quietly.

Maisie tried to find her voice but failed.

"Where have you been?" Rab asked, waving his arms wildly at his pal. "We've been worried sick about you."

"Sorry about that," he said, never taking his eyes off Maisie.

"We need to talk." He took Maisie's frozen hand in his.

"We'll be back before twelve," he told Rab and Chrissie, "bring in the New Year together, if that's alright with you Maisie."

Rab and Chrissie watched as the pair disappeared up Reform Street.

"Where are they going?" Chrissie asked. Rab shrugged and wrapped his arms around Chrissie. "Don't care where they're going," he said huskily, "just as long as you're here with me."

Chrissie snuggled closer to Rab's chest, feeling his warmth surround her.

Now was Rab's moment.

"Chrissie," he said slowly, unwinding her arms from his neck.

"Remember I said I had something for you?"

Chrissie nodded.

With breathing on hold, he took the little box from his pocket and opened it. The diamond ring sparkled in the

Christmas lights swinging overhead from the streetlamps and matched the glistening tears in Chrissie's eyes.

"Do you want to be engaged to me," Rab said shyly, "I mean, officially like?"

Chrissie felt an uncontrollable giggle rising from the soles of her boots and mixing with her tears of happiness.

"I do" she said, her words almost lost in the noise of the crowd.

Rab pulled her nearer as he slipped the ring on her finger.

"Say that again," he said, all anxiety now disappearing.

"I do," shouted Chrissie, before Rab's lips found hers.

1963 was going to be wonderful.

Purposefully, Kenny led Maisie to one of the wooden slatted benches that were dotted around the Albert Museum. The crowd had thinned considerably here and it seemed that there was no else in the world besides themselves.

"Do you forgive me Maisie," Kenny asked quietly, "for being such an idiot?" Maisie's eyes widened. "ME forgive YOU," she said, breathlessly, "isn't it me who should be asking you for forgiveness?"

Kenny smiled. "I'm not talking about Ian Brown," he said, "I know that nothing happened between you two." Maisie felt her breathing ease.

"I mean forgive me for not realising the needs of the beautiful woman beneath the blonde mop." He ruffled Maisie's curls gently and kissed her forehead. "But now I do."

"I don't understand," Maisie began to say, but Kenny stopped her.

"Yes you do," he said, determined to let Maisie know he understood her completely. You wanted a better life for yourself and you thought Ian Brown could give it to you," he said frankly. Maisie hung her head, Kenny seemed to know her better than she knew herself.

"I didn't really........"

Again Kenny stopped her. "You haven't done anything wrong Maisie, wanting a better life for yourself. It's what I want too."

Maisie eyes searched his, wondering at how little she really knew the man she had fallen in love with.

He pulled her closer to him trying to still the shivering inside both of them. "Listen carefully, Maisie," he said, turning her face to his. "I spent yesterday with Shug Reilly," he began "and together we went to the Army Recruiting Office." He took the deepest breath of his life. "Maisie, I've signed up for the British Army."

Maisie again was lost for words.

"They can offer me a trade Maisie, in the REME and all and travel to other countries," his eyes misted at the possibilities that now lay before him.

Maisie's elation at having Kenny back and unharmed, disappeared into the darkness of the night. "Does that mean you're leaving Dundee?" she stammered, the bleakness returning to her spirit.

"It means," he said softly, "that WE are leaving Dundee."

"We?" Maisie blinked in disbelief. But Kenny had more to say.

"Will you marry me Maisie Green?" Kenny asked, "for better or for worse and travel the world with me and be a soldier's wife?"

Maisie felt herself dissolve into Kenny's arms, as the world kept turning all around them.

She nodded, her throat so tight she felt she would never speak another word again.

"Is that a yes?" Kenny said, tilting her chin up and brushing a tear from her cheek.

The Green Years

"Yes," Maisie managed to say, just as twelve o'clock chimed all over Dundee.

"Happy New Year Maisie," Kenny whispered, as snow began to fall all around them.

"Now you're a soldier," Maisie giggled, finally finding her voice, "does that mean you have to obey orders?"

Kenny gave her a quizzical look. "It does," he said pulling her to her feet and wrapping his arms around her.

"Then I order you to tell me you love me and ...." but Maisie never managed to say another word as Kenny kissed her again and again. Maisie had at last found 'the one' and 1963 was truly going to be wonderful.

------oOo-----

Printed in Great Britain
by Amazon